AN IMPERFECT CHRISTMAS

Tanya Jean Russell

SAPERE
BOOKS

AN IMPERFECT CHRISTMAS

Published by Sapere Books.

20 Windermere Drive, Leeds, England, LS17 7UZ,
United Kingdom

saperebooks.com

ISBN: 978-1-80055-139-8

CHAPTER ONE

'Some abnormalities have shown up in your cervical screening. Please make an appointment with your doctor as soon as possible.' As the voicemail message ended, twenty-five-year-old Maggie Green felt her pulse racing.

Just breathe, the familiar voice in her head said. Habit forced a gulp of oxygen into her lungs, but did little to control her rolling stomach.

Slipping the phone into her pocket, she pressed her toes into the parquet flooring. Resting her now empty palms on the cold metal frame holding the glass of the floor-to-ceiling window, she tried to focus on the city that lay spread out in front of her, pushing the words from her mind.

The drab greyness that could only be London in November greeted her gaze. Too soon for the twinkle of festive lights to catapult the mood into the buoyancy of Christmas, the gloom remained unbroken. The mass of buildings that rolled from below her new eighteenth-storey apartment to as far as she could see wavered, as though the entire apartment block was swaying.

It was just a phone call; a phone call didn't have the power to change your life, only what came afterwards could do that. Afterwards would have to wait. If she was going to fall apart, it wasn't going to be while her boyfriend was in her apartment. She'd spent years building a reputation for being calm, consistent and reliable, as close to perfect as was possible. She wasn't about to let a phone call change that.

Just breathe.

"Maggie, I'm going to make myself a coffee, do you want one?" Rupert's voice broke through the haze of emotion.

"No thank you." The words came out without any conscious instruction from Maggie's brain, and her eyes flickered down to her pocket. There was no way she was going to keep anything down.

The noise of the expensive coffee machine Rupert had told her she *just had to have* spluttered to life, the sound seeming to reverberate through her soul.

Just breathe.

Forcing her shoulders back, Maggie shoved hard against her brain's effort to rerun the brief phone conversation. Now wasn't the time to deal with that. She needed to focus, to be calm.

Once she was certain her legs would cope with the small walk to her kitchen, she rubbed at her face and moved.

"I'll miss you," she said, finding a smile at the sight of Rupert, his immaculately styled dark hair glinting in the light as he leant forward, filling a disposable coffee cup and placing the lid on top as he did whenever he stayed over. She'd long since stopped using the cardboard cups, much preferring the reusable flask her niece, Evie, had sent for her birthday, but Rupert had insisted on keeping a stock of them for whenever he stayed over.

Rupert was looking at her as he pulled on the cuff of first one shirt sleeve and then the other, making sure they were perfectly aligned with the suit jacket sleeves and each other. The action, one she knew well from the number of client meetings they'd done together, made her pause.

"We'll only be apart for six weeks," she said, giving him a small smile.

Unfortunately, instead of his smooth shaven features shifting into the amused look he only ever gave her, they shifted into something designed to appear softer.

"Don't give me that look, Rupert." Her voice was clear and steady despite her already turbulent stomach sinking further.

"What do you mean?" he asked neutrally.

"You know what look — you're looking at me the same way you look at clients when you're going to tell them something they don't want to hear."

She didn't really need to say it; there was no way he didn't already know exactly what she was talking about. He'd bragged about how hard he'd worked to perfect *the look*, but she hadn't become as successful as she was without being able to call people out on the things they'd rather you forgot.

"I'm not one of your clients."

"We've had fun, Maggie, but I think we both know this has run its course," he said, gesturing between them.

He was standing in her kitchen after spending the night in her bed, and now he was telling her it was over? She was still in her dressing gown, for goodness' sake. A voice in the back of her mind was trying to tell her she should be far more upset about all of this than she was, but she didn't have the capacity to listen to that voice right now. With almost no effort at all, she pushed back the faint whisper of a scream attempting to escape. She was going to be calm.

"I'm going away to help out at the old family firm and you're breaking up with me? I'll be back in six weeks." She wasn't really sure why she was debating it with him, but the words just kept spilling out. "What about when I'm back at work? It's not like we can just ignore each other when we're both about to be promoted to Director."

Maggie forced her mouth shut. It was as though the phone call had pushed her to her limit and there was nothing left.

"Ah, well, about that," Rupert said, his expression turning sympathetic. "I'm afraid that's not going to work out either."

"What?"

Rupert stepped around her without answering, as she turned to watch him walk to his briefcase and open it. Pulling out a letter, he passed it to her without a word.

Unable to stop herself, Maggie opened it carefully, easing the top so she wouldn't create the jagged edges that bothered him.

The moment the word 'redundant' jumped off the page, the rest of the text disappeared in a blur.

"They're making me redundant?"

"The firm felt they had to make some cutbacks. I'm sorry to be the bearer of bad news, but I thought you'd prefer me to tell you privately."

Maggie stared at the paper without seeing anything. Getting another job wouldn't be a problem, not with her reputation, but she'd been so close to making director. Now she was going to have to start all over again. Surely this couldn't be happening? Her boss Henry had been talking about her bright future just yesterday.

"What are we going to do?" she asked, turning her eyes to Rupert's dark ones.

He shifted almost imperceptibly, a movement she'd certainly have missed if it hadn't been for months of working side by side every day, and sleeping side by side most nights.

"Ah, well, that's the thing — it's just you," he said, giving her that polished look of concern again. He shifted again, as though he was planning to step towards her.

Lifting an arm, Maggie shook her head. She might not know where to begin processing this, but she knew there was no way he was going to touch her. There was no way she could hold it together if he did.

"I think you should leave," she said, determined not to let the flood of emotions out while he was still in her flat.

"You're right, I don't want to be late," he said, carefully straightening his cuff again after checking the gold watch on his wrist. He watched her intently, as though hoping to see some glimmer of the meltdown he clearly thought should be inevitable as he pulled his coat on and headed out of the door.

"I'll leave your things with the doorman so you can collect them while I'm away," Maggie said calmly, trying not to register that her determination to prove she could hold herself together was manifesting in a way that let him off the hook as one thought ran through her head on a loop.

How the hell was she going to face everyone at home now?

CHAPTER TWO

Bitterly cold air whipped around Maggie as she stepped out from the heat of the train and onto the empty platform at Honeyford station. Pulling the belt of her red woollen coat tighter, her icy hand brushed against the letter in her pocket. It had been two years since she'd been home, and another three before that since she'd been back for Christmas. Clearly she'd forgotten just how cold late November was when you ventured outside of London.

The red brick stationmaster's house was still boarded up, but remained graffiti-free. The timber valance of the platform shelter, a greying shade of white, was in desperate need of a touch-up, but looked solid enough. Planters with knee-high shiny silver Christmas trees sticking out at wonky angles were the only sign that the locals were still trying to fight the ravages of time. A losing battle without the funding that had been cut by the local council years ago, although the fact they'd managed to keep the station open at all was a testament to their determination. Despite the fact the place didn't look anything like the picture perfect village station it had once been, a flicker of excitement remained. She was home.

Turning her head, she took in the worn and battered bench positioned against the stone of the abandoned house. The image of that bench was so engrained in her mind that it tried to haunt her despite the passage of time. Hurling her back to another day, another train.

"Here you go," Dean Parker said, his voice almost lost over the rumble of the train and the wind that tunnelled its way down the platform.

Turning to see her old friend's tall frame leaning out of the open doorway, she smiled. He had one hand hanging on to the handle inside the carriage, the other reaching out with her bright turquoise suitcase.

Grabbing it from him with a smile, Maggie promptly staggered half a dozen steps before finally managing to right herself. Turning to help Dean with his bag, she found him next to her on the platform, his eyes bright with amusement.

"Don't laugh."

"I can't believe you brought so much with you for a few weeks," he said.

She frowned at her heavy case, not quite able to believe it either. She'd started with the best of intentions, but somehow every pair of shoes she owned had crept into the case. "It's sensible to be prepared."

Yes, that was definitely all it was. It certainly had nothing to do with nerves about coming home. Absolutely nothing to do with being at home with the Parkers in residence next door, *all* of the Parkers.

"Come on, let's go see who's here to pick us up," Dean said, wheeling her case out to the main road, his own weekend bag slung across his shoulders.

Squaring her shoulders, Maggie followed him. Glad of the respite from the wind as they rounded the corner of the broad building, bringing the small car park into view, she grinned. Trimmed with wild hedges, the cracked tarmac of the car park was empty, except for a single, battered, blue Volvo estate.

"How is that thing still running?"

The vehicle was as much a part of her childhood as Dean's, but it had been on its last legs before she'd moved away. The fact it was still going now was nothing short of miraculous.

"It might look like the same car on the outside, but I think Chris has replaced just about every part under the bonnet," Dean said.

"I know your brother is a good mechanic, but surely it would have been cheaper to buy a new car?"

"You know what Dad's like," Dean said, the warmth in his voice at his dad's dislike of new things coming through clearly, despite the roar of the train that had begun to pull out of the station.

"Dean, Maggie, how was the journey?" Arthur asked, his voice booming as they reached him.

"It was great, Dad," Dean answered, pulling his dad in for a hug before he could grab the cases to put in the car boot.

"Maggie, how is my baby girl?" Arthur asked, his expression serious as he turned to face her. "It's been too long since you came home."

He wrapped his arms around her and lifted her onto her tiptoes. Most of his sons had inherited his deep red hair, and they had all inherited his height. In his mid-sixties, he was still as physically imposing as ever. Maggie let herself enjoy the warmth of the hug from a man who was like a surrogate father. A familiar scent of wood and oil filled her senses as she buried her face into a bobble-covered woollen jumper. Knowing that self-preservation meant she'd had no choice but to cut herself off from this wonderful man and his family didn't stop her from admitting just how much she had missed them.

Coughing to clear her throat, she blinked hard. "It's freezing," she said, giving Arthur a smile as she pulled back.

"Of course, of course. Let's get you both in the car." He hefted her suitcase into the boot in a smooth motion before ushering them into the car.

Strapping herself into the rear passenger seat, Maggie looked up to see Arthur glancing between them, his expression serious.

"I'd better warn you, Agnes is so excited that you are both coming home that she's been baking."

"You're up first, Maggie," Dean said, letting out a bark of laughter.

"Oh, um, that's nice," she said, attempting a smile, stomach churning at the memory of the last time she'd had to eat the Parker granny's cooking. "Um, is it the turkey and sherry scones again?"

"I don't think so," Arthur said, grinning at the pair of them.

Maggie's smile eased into something that felt more genuine as she sank back into the car seat.

"She took a bottle of advocaat through to the kitchen this morning, though," he added as he started the engine up and then headed for home.

As Arthur pulled up outside their homes, Dean turned and smiled at Maggie.

"Ready?"

For a moment Maggie couldn't respond; instead she stared at the two houses side by side, her childhood home sitting exactly where it always had, right next door to the Parker farm house. The farm house was bigger, but the sight of the cottage she'd grown up in pulled at her heart. Trellis framed the front of the cottage, but instead of the roses that covered it throughout the summer it now twinkled with white lights that glowed warmly, pushing back the deepening shadows as the last of the daylight faded.

Despite it being too early for the creation to survive all the way through Christmas intact, the wooden door, painted the familiar muted red, held a holly garland dotted with red flowers. She knew Sarah would have made it with Evie, just as the two of them had done with their mum, and as Sarah had made with Maggie every year after Mum wasn't around. The two sisters had been through so much here, but this was still home. It would always be home. She'd been a fool to let the past keep her away.

Turning to Dean, she smiled broadly. "Yes, I'm ready."

The truth of her statement sank into her bones. She'd spent long enough licking her wounds. She was truly ready to be home. Now she just needed to get through the next few weeks without anyone knowing what a wreck her life had become.

"Good, see you later, then," Dean said, squeezing her shoulder before pulling her case from the boot and setting it on the ground.

"Thanks," she said. A tightness flickered in her chest at the reminder of the gathering at the Parker house that evening, but her joy at being home was undiminished.

Pulling her case, she headed towards the front door, her heart lighter with the anticipation of seeing her family.

As she reached for the handle, the door was flung open and a mass of blonde curls flew out.

"You're here. I can't believe you're here." Evie screeched as her skinny arms were flung around Maggie's waist. "Mummy, Auntie Maggie is here."

"Hey, how's my favourite niece?" Maggie asked, lifting Evie up and hugging her tightly.

"I'm your *only* niece, silly," Evie laughed.

"Doesn't make it any less true."

"Come on, come and see Mummy and Daddy," Evie said, pulling Maggie into the house.

As they reached the kitchen, Sarah came out, drying her hands on a tea towel, her hair a riot of curls that made her look as though she could have been the younger one, though she was actually eight years older than Maggie.

"You made it."

Maggie flinched at Sarah's tone but didn't defend herself; she couldn't exactly blame her sister for being so surprised. "I wouldn't miss your wedding."

"Welcome home, Maggie," said Paul, his greeting much warmer than his fiancée's as his blonde head appeared above Sarah's from in the kitchen.

"Thanks, Paul."

"Come on, pumpkin, time to get your room tidied up," he said to Evie.

"Oh, Daddy, I don't want to. Auntie Maggie just got here," Evie said, whining her response.

"You'll have plenty of time with Auntie Maggie later. Besides, if you want to come to Granny and Grandad's later, you need to tidy your room first. I'll come and help you."

"Okay," Evie said, her shoulders falling with the realisation she wouldn't be able to argue her way out of it.

"You two have a nice catch up," Paul said, planting a kiss on Sarah's head before he disappeared with Evie.

Maggie stood awkwardly under her sister's gaze. Now she was here, she realised she didn't know how to do this. How was she supposed to be a grown up with the sister who had raised her? The fact that Sarah didn't move, didn't fidget with the tea towel or even shift her feet made it worse. She simply stood quietly, watching, exactly as she had always done when Maggie was growing up.

Maggie swallowed hard and decided to just say the words that were swirling around in her head. "I missed you."

Before Maggie realised it, they had closed the distance between them and were hugging, laughing and crying all at the same time.

"I missed you too, Maggie."

"I should have come back sooner."

"No," Sarah said, pulling back enough to look her in the eye. "You came back when it was right for you, but I'm glad it was finally time."

"Thank you for coming to visit me in London," Maggie said.

"You're welcome," Sarah replied. "Ready to tell me why you've been avoiding being here for so long?"

At the concern in Sarah's voice, Maggie's stomach twisted. She had never told her sister what had happened. She never wanted to have to admit what a fool she had been, but she should have known her sister would never have bought the fact she had been too busy to visit. Some part of her had always known the time would come when she'd have to be honest about why she had stayed away.

"I will, but not today," Maggie said quietly.

"Before you go again?" Sarah asked, her tone making it clear it wasn't really a question.

"Yes. I promise," Maggie said, feeling sick that she'd caused her sister to worry.

"Come on then. Let's get a glass of something before we have to go next door," Sarah said.

Taking her coat off, Maggie's hand instinctively went to the letter in her pocket, making sure it wasn't going to fall out. She draped her coat over a kitchen chair as Sarah poured her a generous glass of wine.

Taking the glass, she raised it towards Sarah. "To my amazing sister for finally coming to her senses and agreeing to marry the man who has worshiped her for years."

Sarah laughed. "I wanted to make him work for it."

"I think you might have taken that a little too far. You guys have been together since you were eighteen. Evie is ten. I think he's worked hard enough."

"All right, all right. I've said yes now, haven't I?"

"What changed your mind? It's not like he hadn't asked enough before," Maggie asked.

"Honestly? When he first proposed, I couldn't cope with it. I felt like the world was pressing in on me. Everything had changed and I couldn't deal with being responsible for someone else." Sarah gave a half smile to take the sting out of her words.

Maggie fought to keep her expression light. That first proposal had been six months after their parents had died, fourteen years ago. Six months after Sarah had taken on parental responsibility for her little sister. "I'm sorry," she said. "I know how much you gave up for me."

Maggie swallowed on the old guilt. She'd been eleven when their parents had died in a car accident. As they were travelling back from a rare evening out, a lorry had slipped on a patch of black ice and ploughed into their car. With the passenger seat taking the brunt of the impact, their mum had died instantly. Their dad had died just days later from his injuries. At nineteen, Sarah had refused to let anyone take Maggie away. Making all the necessary legal arrangements, her sister had become her guardian. Sarah had had to grow up and become an adult overnight.

"Don't you dare," Sarah said, waving her coffee cup towards Maggie. "You're my sister and I love you. I just couldn't say yes to Paul then. I was scared he was just asking because he thought he should. I couldn't be responsible for his happiness as well."

"Fair enough, but what about after you had Evie?" Maggie asked.

"I wasn't about to get married just because I was pregnant! God, I was already enough of a small town cliché; letting him marry me to save my reputation was more than I could handle," Sarah said, taking a huge swig of her wine.

"But he moved in," Maggie said with a laugh, moving to pick up her own glass.

Sarah opened her mouth to reply, but the melodic tone of Maggie's phone sounded through the small kitchen.

They both glanced towards Maggie's handbag.

"You should get that," Sarah said when Maggie didn't move.

Heart pounding, Maggie opened the bag; it could be work calling to say they'd made a mistake. Could she be lucky enough that the whole mess would be fixed before anyone found out about it? Probably not. Glancing at the screen, she registered the name of her GP surgery. Hand shaking, she hit the volume button at the side, silencing the relentless tune that was far too cheerful for the call that was attempting to come through. Taking a breath, she shoved the phone back into her bag without answering it.

"Nothing important," she said, finding a smile from somewhere as she turned back to face her sister. "Now, you were telling me why you finally said yes to Paul."

"Ah, you know, I just figured I'd said no so many times he'd stop asking if I wasn't careful."

Maggie knew she should be more concerned about what had happened to change her sister's mind, but all she could think about was that call. She was smart enough to know she couldn't ignore it forever, but maybe just for today.

"So, just three weeks until you're Mrs Parker," Maggie said.

"How crazy does that sound?" Sarah said, the beaming smile on her face making it clear that she was more than ready to face her own future.

"It sounds wonderful."

CHAPTER THREE

Staring at the wooden front door of the Parker home, Maggie wavered. She'd avoided the awkwardness of coming around earlier with Sarah, Paul and Evie by saying she wanted to unpack before eating, but she couldn't stay away forever.

She was expected and she was going to have to suck it up. If she couldn't get through one evening, she had no chance of getting through the next few weeks, and she had to do right by Sarah.

Light spilled from almost all of the windows, but with the single-glazing already misted as the glass held the heated air from inside against the icy cold outside, even those without closed blinds were impenetrable. The sounds of people enjoying themselves drifted out to her. Raising her hand, Maggie knocked determinedly, the bang of her fist louder than she'd intended.

Shivering as she waited for someone to let her in, she tried to ignore the strange sensation worming through her. Maybe he wouldn't be there. Just because he'd moved back didn't mean he would be here tonight. According to Dean he had his own place on the outskirts of the village so he could have stayed home, or he could have other plans.

At the sound of the handle being turned, Maggie held her breath, and quickly let it out at the sight of Grace, her hair in a sleek blonde bob that was streaked with more silver than the last time Maggie had seen her.

"Whatever are you doing waiting out here?" Grace exclaimed.

"I didn't want to assume," Maggie muttered, feeling foolish for not just wandering in as she had been doing her whole life. The easy comfort she'd always felt flitting between the two houses was gone, but it was clear Grace had no idea why. Knowing that, even after all this time, Nathan hadn't told his mum about what a fool she'd been soothed Maggie. At least she wouldn't have to face Grace's pity.

"My goodness, aren't you funny. I don't want you knocking on this door again, do you hear me? You are as welcome here as any of my boys. Just come in whenever you want."

Maggie felt her eyes prickling and she pulled Grace's slight figure in for a hug. The familiar smell of cinnamon and the heavy scent of the perfume Grace had been wearing for as long as Maggie could remember catapulted her back to her childhood — to running into this house for cookies, being held after her parents died, being made a part of the Parker family. She needed to get a grip. In the less than three hours she'd been home she'd had more hugs, and fought off more tears, than in the last couple of years.

"It's good to have you back, princess," Grace said.

Maggie smiled at the use of her old nickname; she couldn't remember the last time anyone had called her that, but a warm glow unfurled as she heard it again.

As Grace bundled her into the house, Maggie accepted the glass mug of mulled wine that was pressed on her.

"Take that into the sitting room and get yourself warmed up," Grace said, her tone making it clear exactly how such a tiny woman had controlled five boisterous boys.

Registering the buzz of conversation coming from the dining room, Maggie was pleased to do as she was told — any excuse to delay the inevitable was welcome. Shoulders relaxing a fraction at the reprieve, she smiled at Grace before heading to the sitting room.

The large but cluttered room was completely unchanged, even the faded throw that Grace had been using to cover up the stains one of the boys had left on the armchair was still in place, although the tassels were even more frayed than Maggie remembered. Grace had always managed to make the space feel cosy. The fire that was currently roaring helped, but this room had always made Maggie feel at home, even when the fire wasn't on.

Approaching the enticing flicker of flames, Maggie suddenly realised she wasn't alone. A figure leaned forward from the large wing-backed armchair and smiled.

He was here. Maggie had had far too much caffeine on the train. That had to be the cause of her suddenly pounding heart, her shaking hands. It certainly couldn't be because of the sight of that oh-so-familiar smile.

Unable to move, she watched Nathan unfold himself from the low-slung armchair. Why couldn't the last five years have made him fat? Instead, his teenaged figure had filled out attractively. Gone was the mismatch of a body so skinny it couldn't fill his broad frame. Now those wide shoulders were full, leading the eye down an equally solid chest, and arms that seemed to radiate power. Those blue eyes had no right to twinkle so appealingly. That face should not have squared up so that the full firm lips that had looked oversized growing up now fit perfectly. The only thing that remained totally unchanged was his auburn hair. It looked as though he'd just climbed out of bed. Her head filled with the heated images that years of fantasies had cemented in her mind.

"Wow," Nathan said softly. "You look amazing."

The familiar rumble of his voice sent an unwelcome jolt right to Maggie's core. She opened her mouth to reply but nothing would come out. Standing, working her jaw up and down, she was aware that she looked like a demented fish, but despite planning this moment for months she couldn't find the words.

Nathan took a step towards her, looking for all the world like he was going to reach out and touch her. She didn't want him to hug her, a fact that her body was merrily ignoring, her foot moving, taking a step forwards as if to meet him halfway. Somehow all sense and reason had vanished, like the smoke that was swirling up the chimney.

"There you are." Dean's voice broke the tension of the moment. Walking to Maggie's side, Dean slung an arm around her shoulders. The contact shook her from her stupor as the silent support eased the tightness in her chest.

Nathan's gaze clouded as he looked from his brother back to her. "Dean," he said, the word flat as he studied her intently.

"Last time I checked," Dean said, with a laugh before turning his gaze from his brother to Maggie. "Here, Mum said you'd arrived so I brought you a few nibbles."

Maggie turned, blinking hard as she broke from Nathan's gaze. She smiled at the sight of the plate of buffet food in Dean's outstretched hand. She didn't want to deal with the myriad of emotions she was feeling, so she focused on the plate piled high with all her favourites. She loved buffet food; it was one of the few times she let herself eat whatever the hell she fancied, and she and Dean had been to enough of each other's work functions together over the last few years that they knew what each other liked.

She grabbed the plate from him with a grin, and slipping out from under his arm sank into one of the couches to start eating. The two brothers didn't move, but stood staring at each other. Nathan's posture was as tense as Dean's was relaxed.

Maggie decided to ignore them. At least if she had food in her mouth she couldn't be expected to make conversation.

Within moments everyone who had been in the dining room had piled in, sitting on every available seat and sprawling across the rugs. With the buzz of mingled conversations, the risk of any kind of personal conversation with Nathan passed safely.

"So how are you settling back in, Nathan?" Dean asked.

"Good, it's nice to have roots again," he said.

"Not missing all those bikini-clad women?" Chris, the second eldest Parker brother, asked with raised eyebrows.

"Yeah, not like you'll get that here, more like padded coats and bobble hats," Joe, the youngest Parker boy commented, before getting an elbow in his ribs from his girlfriend Kate.

"Stop teasing your brother," Grace said. "It's been years since we've all been together. Don't go spoiling it by falling out."

"Sorry, Mum," a chorus of men's voices replied, their heads dipping at the reprimand.

"Seeing as I'm not stuck sharing a room with you, I assume you're staying at your place now?" Dean asked Nathan.

Maggie watched as Nathan glared at his brother before sidestepping the question, instead asking if there were any of the mini steak pies left. She frowned; it wasn't as though staying at his own place would be a big secret.

"Has anyone tried my scones?" Agnes piped up.

A chorus of *ums* filled the room as everyone shuffled and tried to pretend that they were full.

"You'll have one, won't you, Maggie?" Agnes said, grinning at her.

Maggie sank into her chair. There wasn't a chance in hell she could say no to Agnes, but she really, really didn't want to.

"This is my third," Sarah piped up, spitting crumbs as she spoke. "They are amazing. You should all try one."

Maggie looked at her sister in amazement. How on earth did she manage to look so genuine saying that? Regardless, her words were enough to distract Agnes's laser-like focus from Maggie.

"Oh, I am glad. It was a devil of a job finding fresh pilchards to go with the advocaat."

Maggie swallowed hard. Pilchards? In a scone? She was going to owe Sarah for getting her out of that.

"Lucky escape," Dean whispered in her ear with a chuckle.

"God yes," she whispered back, determined not to bring attention back her way again.

"You're glad you're here, though?" he asked.

Maggie looked up, taking in the suppressed laughter of her small family, and the Parkers. The feeling of being home, being back with the people she loved, caused a warmth that she hadn't realised she'd missed so much.

"I am," she said, surprised to realise how much she meant it.

CHAPTER FOUR

Nathan tossed a damp tea towel into a basket in the corner before pulling a fresh one out of the drawer. Despite the fact he'd put a dishwasher in when he'd redone his parents' kitchen on a visit home a couple of years earlier, his mum still insisted on handwashing everything — a massive task with everyone home for the weekend. Right now, though, he was grateful for the excuse to get away from everyone else as they played charades. Not that he had anything against charades, it was just that if he had to look at Dean, sitting smugly his arm around Maggie, who was steadfastly ignoring him, for one more second, he was liable to punch something, or someone.

"Why don't you stay here tonight?" Grace asked, breaking into his thoughts.

"Nah, I'm going to head home soon," he replied.

It was nice to know that he could crash here whenever he wanted, but Nathan needed his own space tonight. He needed some room to figure out what was going on in his head, and that wasn't likely to happen if he had to share a room with Dean. He'd been looking forward to seeing Maggie again this weekend. What he hadn't been expecting was the look on her face when he'd spoken to her. He wasn't naïve enough to think they'd be best mates again straight away. After all, he did still need to apologise, but damn it, the expression on her face had been a haunted mirror of the shock it had shown all those years ago.

He'd been struggling to settle since coming home, despite the fact the renovations on his place were going well and his business was booming. He'd been hoping seeing Maggie again, having his friend back in his life, would fill that final empty space inside of him. Now it looked like that was going to be harder to achieve than he'd anticipated. The fact she hadn't forgiven him, despite the years that had passed, left him feeling hollow. He was going to have to talk to her, find a way to get her to forgive him.

He looked up at the sound of someone coming into the kitchen only to see the woman in question holding a tray full of empty mugs.

"Um, I thought I would bring these through while they get the teams reorganised," Maggie said, tilting her head towards the lounge.

Nathan's jaw tightened; he hated seeing her so awkward. He wanted his old Maggie back, the one who would skid down the wooden halls with him in her socks. The one who would throw a sheet over herself, convinced she could make the older kids believe she was a ghost. The Maggie he was with when they got drunk for the first time, on schnapps stolen from the cupboard under the sink of this very kitchen. Not this corporate-looking withdrawn woman, unsure of herself and her place in a house that had always been her home as much as it had ever been his.

"Thanks, Maggie," Grace said. "You haven't seen the kitchen since it was done, have you? Do you like it?"

Maggie stepped further into the room and took her time looking around. "It's lovely," she said, walking up to the nearest cabinet and stroking her hand across the heavy oak surface.

"Nathan made it for us," Grace said.

Nathan shifted, rubbing the back of his neck with his palm as he watched Maggie taking in his work. He had never thought the day would come that he'd be embarrassed in front of Maggie.

"It really is beautiful," she said as she continued to run her hands along the units he had polished for so many hours that they glowed with a natural finish. They were the first words he'd heard her utter since she came round a few hours ago that sounded natural, and a small part of him warmed at her obvious appreciation of his efforts.

"He's so talented, I just know the old barn will be beautiful when he's finished," Grace added.

The budding warmth inside shrivelled and died as Nathan winced at the words, and at the way Maggie's head jerked around to look at him. He had wanted to tell Maggie about the barn himself.

"The old barn on Castle Hill?" Maggie asked, her voice once again distant.

Nathan opened his mouth to reply but couldn't find the words. How could he explain to her that he had bought the place they had always dreamed of owning together, without her? Oblivious to the undercurrent, his mum carried on.

"Yes, he bought it in the summer. He's managed to get running water and electricity sorted, which apparently means he can live there in one room rather than staying here with us. It's big enough for his business and a home. Even a family home one day, hey, Nathan." Grace nudged him with her elbow, before plunging her hands back into the soapy water.

"Mum." The word came out on a groan as heat flamed up Nathan's face. She could still embarrass him as easily as she had when he'd been a teenager. Taking in Maggie's paling face, he instantly forgot his own feelings. He had wanted to tell her about his plans himself, wanted to explain, apologise.

"Um, I'd better get back," Maggie mumbled as she backed out of the kitchen, and stumbling at the doorway she caught herself before disappearing without a backward glance.

"Catch up or I'll run out of draining board space," Grace said, forcing Nathan's attention back to her as he was debating the wisdom of following Maggie.

Standing in silence, his brain whirring too fast for him to be able to achieve anything, Nathan said a silent thanks for the repetitive task in front of him. Despite his best efforts, one thought kept popping to the front of his mind, and before he could stop himself the words escaped. "Are Dean and Maggie together?" He wanted to curse himself for asking, but the need to know was too strong.

"I'm not sure. Sarah said Maggie was seeing someone, but Maggie hadn't told her anything about him, and you know what Dean's like when it comes to sharing things. I know they go out together quite a lot in London." Grace paused, hands motionless in the water. "I like to tease you boys about grandchildren, but I don't want to interfere. They will tell us when they are ready."

"So you think they are?" Nathan asked, not really sure why he was pushing it when it was obvious his mum thought that was the case.

"Yes, I suppose I do," Grace replied. "Just don't let your granny hear you speculate, though. They'll never get a moment's peace if Agnes finds out, and that poor girl will do the sensible thing and run. Anyway, let me wrap up some leftovers for you to take home."

"Mum, I'm twenty-four, I can feed myself."

"Yes, instant noodles and microwave dinners," she said. "You need proper food."

As Grace proceeded to list the selection of food she was planning to send him home with, Nathan let his thoughts wander. There was no use trying to dissuade her, and if he was honest he was more than happy to take it — his mum's cooking was brilliant. Without having to focus on conversation, his thoughts went back to Maggie. He needed to find an opportunity to speak to her alone. If she was with Dean he'd live with it, but he sure as hell wasn't facing up to his mistakes with one of his brothers watching on.

CHAPTER FIVE

Maggie was trying to focus on the spreadsheet Uncle Walter was talking her through. He wasn't really her uncle, but as her mother's business director he'd been a part of her life for as long as she could remember. Her brain was attempting to absorb a year's worth of accounting work in the two days she had before Walter headed off to Australia for six weeks.

"Are you up to date with the expenses rules?" Walter asked.

Maggie resisted the urge to bristle at the words that made her feel as though she was less than capable of keeping the office running in his absence. In part because she knew he wouldn't even think it. Along with Sarah he'd always been her biggest cheerleader.

"Yes, all up to date," she replied.

"Excellent, you need to keep an eye on Ed Fetheringstone. He brings his accounts in weekly and is always trying to pass off personal items as farm expenses."

Maggie scribbled away in her rapidly filling notebook and nodded. "Weekly?" she asked.

"Yes, quite a few of our clients bring their paperwork in weekly. We encourage it as it helps us manage the workload better."

"So do you do weekly accounts for them?" Maggie resisted the urge to groan on the words. Weekly meant no respite from the deadlines and stress of producing the mountains of required records.

"No, although we do have two clients we provide weekly accounts to. Mostly we just encourage the weekly drop-off so

31

we can work through the paperwork at our leisure, rather than lots of month-end panics."

Although Maggie had done work experience at Frederick & Green accounting, her strongest memories were of watching her mother work there. She had often visited with her dad on her way home from school, or popped in to say hello during the school holidays. Looking at the desk that would be hers in Walter's absence, she had to blink hard against the tears that welled. It had been a long time since her mother had sat there. In that time there had been more junior accountants who'd used the old yew desk, marking the leather surface, covering it with their own marks, than she could remember. Looking at it, though, Maggie wondered if she could really take her mother's place.

"I miss her every day," Walter said, wrapping an arm around her shoulders.

Maggie nodded, her throat itching, not daring to risk speaking, even if she'd known what to say.

"Thank you for doing this," Walter said. "I just don't seem to be able to keep a junior accountant these days. They all want to rush off to the next job as soon as they have a few months' experience."

"They learn so much from you, I think they just want to go and use it," Maggie said, pulling herself together.

"I guess. We just don't have enough work to be able to employ another full-time accountant. I'd really like to go part-time, but until I find someone more reliable there's no chance of that happening."

Taking in the creped furrows of his face, Maggie realised that the passing years were making themselves known to Walter — of course he wanted to find more of a balance in his life. "I hope you find someone," she said softly, slipping her arm around his back and giving him a gentle squeeze. "In the meantime, I'm here to help."

"Are you sure you don't want to reconsider my offer? It would be wonderful to have a Green working here again."

The question was thrown out casually, but Maggie knew the intent behind it was anything but. She paused; in the past she'd never given any serious thought to Walter's repeated offers for her to join the firm. Now, however, she was unemployed. Maybe a job here would be a good idea.

"Maggie's too important to come and work in a little town like this," a voice piped up.

Maggie turned her head to see Susie Lucas, the part time accounts assistant, had come in. Susie was an old friend and Maggie hadn't realised she still worked for Walter. The expression of disgust on Susie's face took Maggie by surprise.

A few years older than her, Susie had been in Dean's year at school, and Maggie and Susie had hung out together sometimes. There was no sign of that old friendship on the woman's face now. Maggie was used to dealing with people who didn't like what she was doing — that was inevitable working in mergers and acquisitions — but the dislike on Susie's face felt personal, and she itched to talk to her and make her like her again. Maggie forced herself to turn back to Walter; they were going to be stuck working together, so there would be time to fix that over the next few weeks.

"My place is in the city," Maggie finally said in answer to Walter's offer.

Whatever was going on with her life, it wasn't fair to use Walter and this place as some sort of back-up plan. Once she'd got the next few weeks out of the way, she was heading back to her apartment and pulling her life back onto the rails she'd been carefully navigating it along.

CHAPTER SIX

Nathan frowned as he watched Maggie carefully folding her long coat and placing it on the back of her chair. Her every move seemed so controlled and calculated that he was struggling to see any sign of the Maggie he'd always known. They'd both had to grow up, but how had she changed so much?

"They've done it up since I was last here," Maggie said looking around, and Nathan couldn't help but turn, taking in the fresh paint and the clean tables, trying to see what she would be thinking of the place. The smell of stale beer mingled now with the scent of the roast potatoes that the landlady always kept a fresh supply of on the bar. The carpet was still the faded green monstrosity of their youth, but the efforts to spruce up the rest of the place had definitely improved things. He suspected it wasn't a patch on the sort of place she and Dean would visit in the city, not if her outfit of tailored trousers and blouse with some sort of long cardigan jacket thing was anything to go by. She definitely looked overdressed surrounded by people in jeans and jumpers.

"I don't really understand the point of a wedding rehearsal," Dean said, breaking into his thoughts as he rubbed his palms together, "but I'm pretty sure they are better when the church isn't freezing cold inside."

"You're not supposed to enjoy it, you're just supposed to be here so you can suffer with the rest of us," Chris said with a laugh.

"Right, drinks are on us but I'm not waiting on you lot all evening, so go and get what you want. Susie's running a tab for us," Paul said, chipping in before Sarah, who looked like she was going to blow a fuse, could get involved.

Joe's face lit up as he turned to see Susie behind the bar.

"And now we all know why Joe came tonight," Dean said, rolling his eyes.

"What, no, what?" Joe said, spluttering the words as his pale complexion flared to a vibrant red.

Nathan looked up to see Susie behind the bar; she and waved at them, her hand and grin falling as Maggie waved back. Looked like not everyone was happy to have Maggie back, Nathan thought.

As the evening wore on, the group began to shrink. Sarah and Paul had long since taken Evie home and Chris had just left with an exhausted Paula. Nathan had enjoyed hanging out with his siblings, but watching Maggie leaning against Dean? Not so much.

"Do you remember that time we stole Mum's gin?" Dean asked.

"Oh my God, that was awful. I don't think I've ever been that ill," Maggie said, her smile making her chocolate eyes glow, pulling him in.

"I don't know, what about that night at the Shard?" Dean gently shoved with his shoulder.

Maggie lifted her hands to her face. "Please don't remind me. I didn't drink anything for months after that."

"Just as well, I don't think that accountant will ever recover."

"Thank God she's not drinking red wine tonight," Nathan said.

Maggie's head swivelled to meet his, her eyes wide as she met his gaze. He realised he'd missed the soft, amused note he'd been aiming for as her expression fell. He didn't imagine either of them could remember the night she'd vomited red wine all down his front without remembering the next night. He wasn't about to address that with an audience, but he'd needed to say something, anything that would remind her that she was supposed to be sitting at his side. He was the one she was supposed to be giggling and reminiscing with.

"No danger of that, she won't touch red wine."

Nathan met Dean's steady gaze and bristled. His brother might not know their history, but the amused curl to his lips gave away the fact he knew exactly what he was doing. Nathan took a long drink from his pint before slamming the nearly empty glass down on the table and standing up. He needed to back up fast before he did, or said, something he couldn't take back.

"Want to play pool, Joe?" He stalked off without looking to check his younger brother was following him.

He should just go home, but despite knowing he had to put some distance between himself and Maggie, he couldn't bring himself to leave her alone with Dean. Snorting to himself, he pulled some coins out of his pocket and slotted them into the side of the table. The dark rumble of balls dropping free within the pool table mechanisms satisfied something inside him.

Racking the balls into place, he broke.

"That's fine, you can go first," Joe said, his voice a drawl of amusement.

Bent over the table, Nathan twisted his head to meet Joe's eyes and stared.

"Jeez, what's crawled up your arse?" Joe asked with a roll of his eyes.

The disadvantage of brothers was they refused to be intimidated by you. Thank Christ it was Joe that had stuck around, though. Nathan knew full well that any of his older brothers would have figured out what was pissing him off within about twenty seconds. At twenty-three, Joe was officially an adult, but despite passing his teenage years some time ago, he still lived in that bubble that all teenagers live in where they only registered the things that impacted them personally.

Missing his shot, Nathan swore. He was good enough at pool that he'd supplemented his meagre earnings by playing when he'd been travelling, but he was completely off his game tonight.

Leaving Joe to continue his winning streak, Nathan headed to the bar to get them both another pint. The magnetic pull to look at Maggie dragged at his insides and, waiting for Susie to finish serving the couple sitting at the other end, he allowed himself a glance over his shoulder.

Maggie and Dean were sitting, their bodies twisted so they faced each other, their heads close enough they appeared to be whispering sweet nothings. As Dean lifted his hand and brushed his fingers under one of Maggie's eyes and then the other, Nathan realised she was crying. Heart pounding, he was half off the stool before he realised what he was doing. She wasn't his to comfort anymore, she hadn't been for a very long time. Scrubbing his hand over his face, he turned his back on them to stare unseeingly at the row of bottles hung on the wall behind the bar.

CHAPTER SEVEN

Hurtling through the front door, Maggie threw her coat onto the bannister before heading for the kitchen. Her heels clicked on the wooden flooring as a quick glance at her watch let her know she should have been back twenty minutes ago.

"Sorry, I just had to wrap up the final weekly account," she said to Sarah, before pulling up short at the realisation Dean and Nathan were both there.

Sarah rolled her eyes. "You're here now, but we'd better get going or we'll be late for the appointment."

Maggie winced; she'd gone into the office at 5am to make sure she'd get the accounts finished and be back in time to head into Bristol for the dress fittings, but she'd still managed to be late. Just for once she'd like to get things right for her sister.

"I've just come to say goodbye," Dean said with a smile. "Why don't you see me out?"

"Hurry up, I've booked us in to that new vegan place as well for dinner afterwards, and apparently if you're even a minute late they release your table."

Maggie resisted the urge to grimace; she was all for trying new food, but she hated anything that contained beans, something she knew was going to make eating in a vegan restaurant almost impossible. Nathan caught her eye with a frown, his mouth opening as though to object on her behalf, but she shook her head subtly. It was one meal, she'd cope.

Dean stood and walked over to Maggie, grabbing her hand and leading her back to the front door before Sarah could object to him delaying them further.

"You sure you don't mind fixing these doors?"

Sarah's voice followed them down the hallway. At Nathan's response, Maggie realised he'd been roped in to fix the loose cabinet doors while they were out. At least that explained why he was there.

Pulling his coat from the mound on the banister and shrugging it on, Dean turned to Maggie, his expression serious. "You're going to be okay."

She leant closer to him to catch the whispered words.

"You know one of the other firms will snap you up as soon as you call them, they've been trying for long enough, and you're better off without Rupert."

"I know, you've told me enough times since the rehearsal." She hadn't intended to tell anyone about the disasters of a few days ago, but a few glasses of prosecco and a sympathetic friend had been all it had taken for everything to come spilling out. The fact that Sarah had drawn attention to her so-called professional success had made her feel like a complete fraud. She was really glad she'd told Dean, though; his unwavering support was just what she needed.

"Yes, well he was a prat. You shouldn't trust a man who uses that much hair stuff."

Maggie laughed and stretched onto her tiptoes to rub her palm against the dark red of Dean's cropped hair. "Easy for you to say." Spinning her head round at a creaking sound, she caught sight of Nathan's head disappearing back into the kitchen.

"And don't worry about my dopey little brother."

Maggie smiled at the amusement in Dean's voice. He didn't know the details but, in her worry about coming home when Nathan was going to be there as well, she'd told him enough that Dean understood Nathan had rejected her at some stage.

"Thanks, Dean," she said, "I'm not sure how I'm going to get through the next couple of weeks without you."

"You'll do great, you always do. Anyway, I'll be back in two weeks for the wedding and to help you torment my brother some more." He gave her a quick hug before shoving her shoulder good-naturedly. "Now go do all that girlie crap for the wedding."

Watching Sarah as she stood on a small pedestal in the sleek column of her wedding dress, Maggie had to blink hard. Her sister looked beautiful; the long sleeves were trimmed with a feathery substance that added to the otherworldly effect of the dress and was matched by the stole that curved around her shoulders.

"You look beautiful," Maggie said, her voice cracking on the words.

Sarah's refection smiled back at her as she studied herself in the full-length mirror.

"A couple of minor alterations to let the fabric out here, and here," Mrs Bellingham said, the words surprisingly clear given the fact she had a mouth full of pins.

Pins that were deftly being poked into Sarah's waist and bust. Pulling the remaining items out of her mouth and dumping them into a tin, she gestured impatiently to Sarah.

"Thank you so much, Mrs Bellingham, it's just perfect."

"Yes, yes, I am a genius and you look beautiful. Now go change, we have to get your bridesmaids done as well."

Sarah rolled her eyes at Maggie, who was doing her best not to giggle at the bossy woman. Leaving Sarah to get herself out of her dress, Maggie drew Evie into the bedroom indicated and helped her to slip into the burgundy tea dress. The cream lace and chiffon overlay stopped the colour from being too harsh for Evie's pale skin and made it look as though she'd been out in the snow.

Leading her niece out to the pedestal, Maggie stood back to let the seamstress, who was grumbling about the rate young bridesmaids grow, do her work.

Slipping her arm around Sarah, she enjoyed the peace of just being together.

"I know she's a bit bonkers, but she's the best dressmaker around," Sarah whispered.

Maggie's phone beeped and she lifted it from her handbag. She was avoiding so many people now that she'd probably be better off ignoring her phone altogether, but she couldn't quite make herself do that. She wasn't sure what that said about her, but she knew it wasn't anything good. Her screen filled with a text from Dean; he'd sent her a meme of a guy slipping in his own hair gel. The image made her smile. He'd always taken the mickey out of Rupert's perfectly styled hair, and seemed to have taken the news of their break-up as an excuse to ratchet that up a notch or ten.

"Something funny?" Sarah asked.

"Just a text from Dean," Maggie said, before changing the subject. The last thing she wanted to do was explain to her sister why the message was funny. "Anyway, *a bit* bonkers? I thought wedding dress fittings were supposed to be sipping champagne in glossy showrooms, not being berated in the doily- and bauble-filled front room of someone's flat."

The room was filled with jars and ornaments that didn't appear to have any kind of theme or colour scheme pulling them together. The furniture even had crocheted arm covers, something she hadn't seen outside of photos of her grandparents' home. The only things that had any consistency throughout the room were the myriad Christmas baubles and ornaments, not that they matched each other, but at least they were all festive. Although it was still November, just, Mrs Bellingham clearly didn't subscribe to the usual rules of waiting for December to arrive before decorating. If Maggie had been shown this room, she'd have bet everything she owned against the region's most stylish wedding dress designer being based here.

"She is getting too tall," Mrs Bellingham muttered. "It's lucky your wedding is less than three weeks away or there wouldn't be enough length for this dress."

Evie twisted so she could look at them over her shoulder and pulled a face.

"And there is the teenager in the making," Sarah said with a laugh.

"God help you when that girl gets more determined," Maggie added. "She's already an expert at getting her own way."

"Hold still, child," Mrs Bellingham snapped, and Evie turned back into position with a roll of her eyes.

"She reminds me of you growing up," Sarah said with a smile.

"What do you mean?"

"You were ready to take on the world. Even after we lost Mum and Dad, you were so brave, if you wanted something nothing would stop you, and look at everything you've achieved."

Maggie swallowed hard. She'd never realised her sister saw her like that. Finding that out when everything she'd achieved had tumbled away from her was bittersweet.

"If she turns out like you, I'll be so proud."

Sarah's words reverberated through her. Evie couldn't turn out like her. The idea of her bright, confident niece growing up to understand that she wouldn't be able to rely on anyone, that everyone would leave her eventually, was like a punch in her gut. She didn't want that for Evie.

"Anyway, enough mushy stuff," Sarah said. "You need to go and put your dress on."

Sarah. Something important curled around the edges of Maggie's mind, something important, but she couldn't quite reach it. In the quiet of the bedroom she shrugged out of her suit and blouse and pulled the dress over her head. A mirror of Evie's dress, the satin fabric brushed her thighs as she walked back to the lounge, and Maggie felt as close to the princess she'd always wanted to be as she could remember.

"I didn't think I'd ever be wearing a dress that was for your wedding," Maggie said, smiling at her sister.

"No need to go on about it. I said yes in the end, didn't I?" Sarah said.

"Hold still," Mrs Bellingham said. "Your dress needs lots of work."

Maggie did as she was told. Peering down to admire the shoes, cream with burgundy glitter-covered heels, she thought they were gorgeous, and couldn't wait to wear them. This was her first fitting after sending her measurements by email months ago, so she wasn't expecting the dress to fit as well as it did. The dress hung a little tight around her hips and chest, but otherwise it was perfect. She resisted the urge to trace the scalloped lace across her collar bone as Evie, now back in her jeans and T-shirt, sang along badly with whatever hit song she had playing on her iPod. Okay, so the setting wasn't glossy and sleek, but this was exactly what dress fittings for a wedding should be: precious moments with your family.

"How did you wangle so much time off from the florists?" Maggie asked Sarah, as her sister chatted through the wedding prep she was planning over the next few days.

"Oh, I stopped working there ages ago. I had a stint at the local nursery after that, and now I'm cleaning at the school," Sarah replied.

"One of these days you'll find a job you like enough to stick at," Maggie said with a frown.

"Oh no you don't," Sarah said with a frown of her own.

"Don't what?" Maggie asked.

"Start with all that guilt about me not finishing my degree again. I'd have hated being an accountant and we both know it."

Maggie swallowed down the guilt that she was basically living the career her sister was supposed to have had. Well, she had been living it until recently. The truth was, she did know that Sarah would hate being an accountant, but it didn't change the fact that she felt guilty for Sarah's lack of direction in relation to work.

Flinching as the ringing of her phone broke her from her darkening thoughts, Maggie met Sarah's eyes in the mirror.

"Hold still, there is lots to do," Mrs Bellingham said as Maggie itched to check her phone.

"Shall I get it for you?" Sarah asked.

Maggie shook her head. She definitely didn't want that. "No, it won't be anything important."

Thankfully, her voice sounded light and relaxed. She forced her shoulders down an inch and pretended not to notice Sarah's frown.

Finally able to step down from the stand and head back to the bedroom, Maggie breathed a sigh of relief. Maybe the call was just someone from the Frederick & Green office. Every phone call wasn't going to be some kind of harbinger of doom. Suit back in place, she smoothed her hair back into its bun and walked to the lounge.

Sarah stood staring at her, phone in hand, face frozen.

"What's wrong? Has something happened? Is Paul okay?" Maggie asked, dashing to her sister's side, words spilling out in a panic at the look of shock on Sarah's face.

As she reached her sister, she registered what she was seeing. Sarah was holding a phone, but it wasn't her own, it was Maggie's.

"When it rang again, I figured someone really needed to get hold of you."

A tremor passed through Maggie; what the hell was that call? The problem with having multiple secrets was that you had no idea which one someone might have discovered.

"Mum?"

Maggie and Sarah both turned to look at Evie.

"What's wrong?"

"Nothing sweetie, Mum and Auntie Maggie just need a quick chat. You keep enjoying your games." Sarah gestured to Evie's iPod.

Evie shrugged and turned her attention back to the small screen, at which point Sarah grabbed Maggie's elbow, dragging her out of the room.

"How could you keep this from me?" Sarah hissed.

Maggie shuffled in place; what the hell was she supposed to say?

"You're ill and you didn't bother to tell me?"

"How do you know that?" She should be remaining calm, downplaying the whole thing, but she couldn't help leaping to defend herself, the way she always had when Sarah had caught her out.

"Don't even try to turn this on me. I picked up your phone and the woman on the other end assumed it was you. They were bleating on about how relieved they were to get hold of you, how important it was you made an appointment with a gynaecological oncology consultant as soon as possible."

"Oh."

"'Oh' doesn't even cover it. Oncology, I know what that is. You could have cancer and you didn't tell me."

The hurt in Sarah's voice sliced through Maggie. She could say she hadn't wanted to spoil Sarah's wedding. She could say she hadn't wanted to worry her, but while that was part of the truth, it wasn't all of it. She'd become so determined to be perfect, not to admit to any kind of flaw, not to need anyone else, that she'd forgotten how to rely on people, including her sister.

Sarah sighed as Maggie remained silent. "Where do you have to go for this appointment?"

"I don't know. I haven't got that far yet," Maggie said.

"Damn it, Maggie, you can't ignore this, you have to make an appointment."

"I will, soon."

"No, you have to promise me you'll make an appointment today." Sarah glanced at her watch, her eyes filling with tears. "Okay, tomorrow, you have to make the appointment tomorrow, and I'm coming with you."

Maggie nodded, blinking against the prickling in her eyes.

"I know I'm being bossy, but I can't lose you as well," Sarah said, wrapping her arms around Maggie. "Whatever happens, we're in this together."

At the familiar words, Maggie tumbled over the edge, her body shaking as her sister held her. Sarah had said those very words at the small moments in Maggie's life, like whenever

Sarah had been summoned to meet with Maggie's teachers because she and Nathan had been causing mischief, and the big ones, like the night they'd been told their mother had died, and the day their father had joined her.

The flicker of a thought that had been tickling on the edge of her consciousness earlier slammed itself to the front of her brain, digging in so deeply that she didn't even try to shake it away. She tightened her grip on her sister. Not *everyone* had left, not yet anyway.

CHAPTER EIGHT

Maggie pushed as hard as she could, laughing with Evie as they swooped back and forth next to each other, competing to see who could get their swing the highest. The days when she'd had to go easy on her niece to let her win were long gone; now it took all of her efforts just to keep up.

"Can we go on the slide next?" Evie shouted. The excitement of being outdoors was shooting her energy levels even higher than usual.

Maggie eyed the slide sceptically. "I'm not sure I'll fit," she said, taking in its narrow width.

"Of course you will. Come on."

Evie leapt off the swing in a move that made Maggie's heart almost stop, despite knowing she and Nathan had done the exact same thing years before.

Her cheeks tingled in the late afternoon air, but the gloves and scarves they had worn at Sarah's insistence kept the worst of the cold at bay. Giggling, she followed Evie up the steps and clapped as Evie slid down so fast she went flying off the bottom, somehow manging to land on her feet.

"This is definitely a bad idea," she muttered as she eased herself into a sitting position. With the metal edges of the slide gripping her bottom firmly, she realised she really was too big to slide down. Gripping each side with determination, she pulled her arms back and eased herself down the slide a few inches at a time. Fortunately, the silky fabric of her trousers helped, although they weren't doing anything to protect her from the icy cold of the metal. By the time she reached the bottom, Evie was bent double, holding her sides as her body shook with amusement.

"You little monster," Maggie teased as she hoisted herself back up and lunged for Evie.

Evie darted out of her grasp and Maggie chased her around the field, weaving as she tried to catch up with her niece.

"You can't escape me forever," she wheezed, trying to distract the girl long enough to have a chance of catching up with her.

"Wanna bet?" Evie giggled.

Blasted child didn't even sound out of breath.

"Fine, I give up," Maggie said as she sat on the bench. "I'm not fit enough to catch you anymore."

Evie ran over and sat with her, the pair of them giggling at their silliness.

"What are you two up to?"

Nathan's voice interrupted their amusement. Maggie looked up to see him standing in running gear. Even with his face red from the combination of exertion and cold, he looked unfairly handsome.

Evie jumped up at his words, throwing herself into her uncle with a *whomph*.

"Steady, pumpkin. You'll knock me over," he said with a smile, catching her easily and spinning her around.

The thought that she wished it was her being spun in Nathan's arms flashed through Maggie's head, and she stamped it down fast. She wasn't about to make the same mistakes again, and yes, she had drunkenly admitted to Dean that she missed Nathan, but that was about missing her friend, nothing more.

"Ooh, that stick looks perfect for a catapult. Will you make one for me, Uncle Nathan? I love catapults. Last time I had one Dad let me line up empty cans and knock them down," Evie chattered away as she ducked down to grab the stick in question. "I'm going to find some more in case this one breaks."

As their niece moved away from them to poke around in the bushes that bordered one side of the park, Nathan sat next to Maggie. The heat of his body seemed to radiate into her side and she held herself awkwardly. Staring at the bare branches of the trees that lined the park, she fished around for something to say, anything to break the silence. They had always been so comfortable with each other whether silent or chattering. Something else to miss. Finally, she blurted out the question she really wanted to know the answer to.

"So you're back for good?"

Steadfastly ignoring his movement as he shifted on the hard bench to look at her, she kept her gaze on the gnarled branch of a tree halfway along one side of the park. It had been hard enough to ask the question; she certainly wasn't feeling brave enough to make eye contact with him as well.

"Yes," he said, holding still for a few beats before finally looking away.

Seriously, that was it? That was all he was volunteering about his plans? About the fact he had bought the old barn? They had dreamed about that place as children, brim full of ideas about what they would do when they were grown-ups and they owned it together. The dreams had started out with them filling the place with thrones, slides and ball pits and ended up with plans for a bar, games room and library, and now he was there alone. Her grown-up self knew it was irrational to be upset that he was doing it without her, but somehow she felt cheated.

"Had enough of seeing the world, then?" She wanted to add *and every woman in it*, but wanted to hang on to her dignity more.

"It was great fun, but I'm done."

"So how many countries did you actually visit?"

"Do you know, I'm not sure?"

He laughed and she found herself laughing along with him. Only Nathan would travel the world and not keep track.

"I started in Europe, going to Croatia, Spain — the usual places — and just kept going."

As he listed all the countries he had visited, Maggie found herself relaxing and enjoying listening to him. His voice was deeper, but it was still so familiar. The cockiness of the teenage boy she had known had been replaced with a solid confidence. Nathan had grown into a man who was sure of himself, and his place in the world.

"So which was the best?" she asked when he had finished.

"Morocco."

"Wow, don't feel like you have to think about it on my account," she said in response to his almost instant answer, shifting her body to face him.

"It was amazing. There is so much poverty, but the people I met were so inspiring."

"What made it so memorable?"

"It's a funny sort of community travelling. Wherever you are, you decide where you want to go next and find people who want to go there as well. I was in Spain and decided I wanted to go to Morocco. I met a couple of Welsh people on a gap year and we went together. On the first day in Casablanca we went to the *souk*. It's basically a market, but the stalls are almost like dodgy, tumbledown sheds crammed against each other. I'm sure the only reason they stay upright is because they are all pressed so closely together they hold each other up.

Stalls are set up in all the walkways and the whole place is a teeming mass of people and activity. The noise seems to swallow you up. The place was a scramble of colours and smells, unlike anywhere I'd been before, or have been since. There were these amazing stalls selling wooden furniture, all hand-crafted and hand-polished to the most amazing shine."

"Like your parents' kitchen," Maggie said, placing her hand on his arm with the realisation.

His gaze travelled to where her palm rested on the thin fabric of his running top and she pulled back, face heating at the realisation she'd slipped back into such an old habit. He didn't comment but simply responded to her statement.

"Exactly. The people I'd travelled with moved on quickly, but I stayed. I spent almost two years there. Working with the locals and learning their craft, helping them make things for their stalls in exchange for food and a roof over my head."

"You sound like you really loved it."

"I did. I moved on eventually because I wanted to see a bit more of the world, but the things they taught me stayed with me. Everywhere I went after that I sought out people who made wooden products and worked for them to learn their techniques. I never stayed anywhere else as long as I had in Casablanca, though."

"So why come home now?"

"I was starting to want a permanent roof over my head. I'd only made it home once in over eight years, and sad as it sounds, I was starting to miss the family. I was missing everyone here." He looked up, attempting to hold Maggie's gaze, but she looked away quickly.

"So what are you doing with yourself now you're back?" she asked, determined to steer clear of anything too personal.

"I've started my own furniture-making business."

He studied his hands as he spoke, as if embarrassed. Her eyes followed his, and she took in the thick fingers and broad palms. Strong hands, the sort that would keep you safe. No, what? The sort perfect for making furniture. That was definitely what she had meant to think.

"Congratulations," she said, and found she really meant it. She was glad he had found his path. The familiar hollowness that she wasn't a part of it seemed to balloon at the reminder, but she was glad he'd found something he loved doing. She loved her career and would be completely lost without it. God, she really hoped she could just walk into something else when she got back home.

"Auntie Maggie, Uncle Nathan, look," Evie called as she headed back towards them, her arms so full of sticks that only her eyes were visible above the pile.

"How many catapults do you think you need?" Nathan asked.

As they stood to help her with her haul, Maggie realised that the light was rapidly fading.

"Come on, we'd better get you back home before your mum thinks I've kidnapped you," Maggie teased.

Nathan walked to the house with them, helping to stow the sticks safely away after Evie had started to worry someone would steal them overnight. As Maggie turned to thank him, Evie cried out.

"Oh no!"

They both turned to see Evie staring at her feet, her expression one of complete distress.

Maggie knelt, holding her niece's hands in hers. They were surprisingly warm in Maggie's own frozen ones. "What's the matter, pumpkin?" she asked, as her exuberant niece began to cry, tears streaking down her face.

"My shoes," she managed to get out between sobs. Maggie's heart squeezed with the need to stop Evie's tears as her eyes followed her niece's gaze.

Taking in the sight of the flashes of cream lace and burgundy satin amongst the layer of mud that had soaked the fabric, her heart sank.

"Are those —" she began.

"Yes," said Evie, her words coming out as staccato sobs. "My wedding shoes. Mum is going to kill me."

Sarah was going to kill them both. How on earth hadn't Maggie noticed that Evie had come out in her bespoke wedding shoes? This was going to stress Sarah out, something her sister really didn't need with her wedding just three days away. She had to figure out a way to fix this.

As her thoughts bounced around without coming to any conclusion, Maggie became aware of Nathan kneeling down next to her, his bare arm brushing against her jacket, almost knocking her off balance as she instinctively flinched to avoid contact. He lifted his hand and gently wiped away Evie's tears with his thumb, leaving smudges of dirt in their wake.

"Come on, pumpkin, we can fix this."

"But it's only three sleeps away. Mum said I couldn't wear them and I did. I'm gonna be so dead."

"And you'd feel sad if you spoilt your mum and dad's wedding, wouldn't you?" Nathan asked, his tone direct.

"I would. It has to be perfect," Evie cried.

"Okay then," Nathan said, turning to Maggie with a smile. "Auntie Maggie and I will fix it."

"How?" Maggie asked, her incredulity clear despite her concerns for her niece. "There is no chance we're getting all that mud out of satin, never mind the cream lace."

"We're going shopping. I'll pick you up at eleven tomorrow," Nathan replied, a smile in his voice as he stood again. "Don't worry, Evie, I promise it will be okay."

He turned and walked across the lawn to his parents' house, whistling as he went, before Maggie could reply.

"But I have to work tomorrow," Maggie called after him, before shaking her head. Never mind, she'd go in early again and get caught up before Nathan came round.

She wasn't anywhere near as confident as he was that they'd be able to replace a pair of bespoke satin and lace shoes in one day, but she pulled a smile from somewhere for Evie. One way or another, she'd have to fix it. She wasn't about to let anything spoil Sarah and Paul's wedding. They had waited long enough and they deserved perfection. If that meant she had to spend time alone with Nathan, well, she'd deal with it.

Evie's hand curled around Maggie's cheek and she smiled, a full, genuine smile.

"Don't worry," she said. "Uncle Nathan promised. He always keeps his promises."

Maggie sighed; her attempted smile was obviously a lot weaker than she had thought. It seemed they would both have to put their faith in Nathan, only she didn't have quite the same faith in the man's promises as her ten-year-old niece.

"Come on then, sweetie, let's get you inside and get those shoes hidden."

CHAPTER NINE

Why had he said eleven a.m.? It was ridiculous to have to wait so long. When he'd thrown out his plan to Maggie yesterday, he had been thinking practically; he had a couple of orders due next week, which with the wedding on Saturday, meant making the most of what time he did have. Unfortunately, despite waking at stupid o'clock, he hadn't made anywhere near the progress he should have. Now he was sitting in his truck, one street away from his childhood home, full of nervous energy and with no clue as to why he hadn't just driven around the corner and popped in to see his mum before he picked Maggie up.

Okay, he wasn't stupid, he knew exactly why he hadn't gone to his parents. It was because he was excited to be spending the day with Maggie, and he didn't want to share that with anyone. Sure, her jaw had fallen open at his assumption she'd agree to go with him, and sure he still had to apologise, but their easy companionship in the park had given him hope that they could get back to where they had been all those years ago. He missed his friend.

Pulling up outside the house, he stopped the truck and started to climb out, but Maggie was already coming. He smiled at the sight of her juggling her bag and two flasks, while trying to close the door behind her. She had been waiting for him. The thought warmed him, and some of his nerves faded. As she walked up the footpath, he moved around the truck and opened the passenger door for her to save her from having to repeat her balancing act. As she reached him, he forced his gaze away from her heeled knee-high boots. They had weird cut outs up the length of them that seemed to reveal the shape of her calves and made him appreciate them more than he should, especially considering how completely inappropriate they were for an excursion in this sort of weather.

Once she was safely inside, he walked back to his side and climbed in, trying hard to shake off the heat those boots had generated.

"Are you sure you're going to be warm enough?" he asked, almost biting his tongue as the question came out. She looked sexy as hell, but it appeared his concern for her had overridden the fact his body wanted her to stay dressed exactly as she was.

She frowned at him before looking down at her clothes and giving him a curt nod.

If it hadn't been for the fact her coat looked warm enough, he knew he'd have had to send her back inside to change.

"Sarah had these in her cupboard, so I made tea," she said. Her change of subject prevented him from persisting. Her gaze focused on the two flasks she held. "I wasn't sure if you still took it white with one sugar. I hope it's okay."

She remembered how he took his tea? With that, the last of his nerves and concerns vanished.

"Perfect, is this mine?" He reached over to take one of the flasks from her. They were only going to be in the car for thirty minutes, but he wasn't about to tease her for being over-prepared, not yet anyway. "Sarah and Paul got them, so they don't freeze while they watch Evie's football matches."

"I haven't seen her play for ages," Maggie said.

"That's a shame. It's the Christmas break, so she won't be playing for a couple of weeks. She's come on loads in the few months I've been home. It's even starting to look like football now, rather than a swarm of kids chasing the ball like bees around a honeypot."

Maggie giggled and the sound filled the car. It was richer than it had been when she'd been a teenager, but it was still unmistakably Maggie, and he couldn't help but join in with her. It was a sound he wanted to hear more of, and he vowed to try to make her laugh as much as he could while she was visiting.

By the time they pulled into the car park outside of the market square, they were chatting easily.

"I haven't been into town for years. Where on earth do we start looking for bridesmaid shoes?"

"Um, I was kind of hoping you would know," Nathan said, grimacing at Maggie. "I know what shops we have, but I have no idea where we would find something like that."

"Okay, teamwork it is, then. Is there a wedding shop?"

"No. I know because we had to travel into Bristol to get our groomsmen suits."

"Shoe shops?"

"I think there are a couple on the high street."

"Well, let's start there and we can keep an eye out for anywhere else that might work as we go."

"Try this one on," Nathan said, holding a hat out to her as he sported a Santa one with flashing baubles. She looked up from the display and, as he'd hoped, laughed, before good-naturedly taking the one he offered her and shoving it on her head. She should have looked ridiculous; the elf hat covered her ears with plastic pointy ones stuck on the side of the green fabric. Her brown hair stuck out at all angles from underneath, yet she looked adorable. She stepped closer, and his breath caught in his chest as she reached up, straightening the hat he was wearing.

"That's better," she said, the words spluttered between her giggles. "Let's get a selfie for Evie."

"You really want to capture this forever?" he asked, gesturing between their heads with his finger.

"Oh yes, Evie will love it, and I'm never letting you forget that look."

She turned her back to him as she fiddled with her phone. He slipped his arm around her shoulders, pulling her close for the photo, and sucked in a breath. Damn, she still felt perfect tucked into his side. He forced himself to smile. He wasn't about to ruin the easy companionship they'd managed to find today by letting her know the closeness was affecting him. Looking into the tiny screen of her phone, he met her wide-eyed gaze. Maybe he wasn't the only one affected?

The moment she'd taken the picture he pulled his arm back, forcing himself to take a step away. He needed to put some distance between them. She might have been his best friend once, but he had a long way to go to reclaim that title, and that was without considering the fact that she seemed to be in a relationship with one of his brothers. He had to ignore the way his body had responded to having her so close and focus on getting his friend back. *That* was the most important thing.

"Please tell me you haven't kept all those embarrassing selfies we used to take?" he asked with a mock grimace.

She gave him the sort of smile that let him know she still had them, and wouldn't hesitate to use them against him.

He gave her a gentle shove and she quickly returned the favour, the awkward moment forgotten.

Nathan was trying to keep the mood light, but they had been in all three shoe shops without any luck, and he was out of ideas. He'd promised Evie, and he didn't make promises he couldn't keep, not anymore. Now it was looking like he was going to let both Evie and Maggie down. His niece would look at him with those puppy dog eyes of hers and he couldn't take it, and he certainly couldn't let Maggie down again.

"How long do you think it would take us to get into Bristol?" Maggie asked, the question confirming the fact she was thinking about giving up as well.

"We don't need to go to Bristol; we'll find something here," Nathan replied with a confidence he didn't feel. Even from here it would take well over an hour to get into the city in normal traffic, never mind during the Christmas period. Making that trip was a real last resort. "We'll find something, don't worry. Why don't we try in there?" He gestured to the toy shop that had opened just a couple of years ago.

Walking in, they both smiled at the sight of MP3 players and computer games crammed in next to wooden blocks and miniature kitchens complete with plastic food and cutlery.

"Look," Maggie called.

Nathan looked up from the bow and arrow set he had spotted to see Maggie heading towards the very back of the shop, and he went to follow her. "Fancy dress costumes! Do you remember that time we dressed up as Woody and Jessie from *Toy Story*?"

"Oh my God! I'd forgotten about that," she said. "I wanted us to go as Cinderella and Prince Charming, but you refused."

"Of course I refused, you always wanted to go as a princess. It was all right when you went as Belle and I got to go as the Beast, but I wasn't going to wear shiny trousers and geek hair."

"You'd have had a sword."

"It would have taken more than a sword to make anyone look manly in that monstrosity."

Nathan joined in her laughter at the memory. Maggie had refused to speak to him for nearly two days when he'd refused to go with the Prince Charming idea. She'd only forgiven him when his mum had come up with the idea of the two characters from *Toy Story*. It felt good to laugh with her again, to think about their past without that sinking feeling he'd become used to over the last few years. He grinned when her initial laughter descended into an uncontrollable giggling fit. Growing up, she'd had moments when she'd laughed so hard neither of them could remember what they'd been laughing about. As tears began to run down her cheeks, she sucked in a breath, finding her control again. He gently wiped the moisture from her face.

"Come on, let's see if they have any shoes for Evie," Maggie said, the warmth of her hand resting on Nathan's forearm pulling his thoughts back to the present.

"No purple satin," he said, his heart sinking as he looked at the selection the shopkeeper had laid out for them to see.

"It was burgundy, but no," she agreed. "Nothing even close." She was holding a bright pink shoe in her hand, turning it so that the light reflected from the diamantes that covered the small heel and the bow on the front, making them sparkle. She looked at them longingly before putting the shoe down. "There are white ones, though. They will be okay," she said, gesturing to the counter at a pair of plain white fabric shoes. They were simple slip-on shoes, and as far as Nathan could tell they looked similar in style to the ones Evie had managed to cover in mud.

He looked from the shoes to Maggie and back again. Gone was the look of pleasure and in its place a resigned acceptance. "We should get the sparkly ones," he said, glancing down at the spectacular boots she was wearing.

She looked up at him in surprise before turning her gaze back to the pink shoes. "No, we can't. The pink is the wrong shade and it's too different from the original shoes," she said eventually.

It was the pause that did it. Maggie wanted to get the sparkly shoes, and Nathan might not have seen her for years, but he suspected she still wanted to dress up as a princess. Time to get this done.

"What shoes do you think Evie would like best?" he asked, knowing full well that his niece would adore the sparkly ones.

"Normally, she'd want the princess shoes. Every little girl wants to feel like a princess sometimes," Maggie said, gesturing to the sparkly shoes. "Even grown-up girls want to feel like a princess occasionally," she added, so quietly Nathan was certain he was supposed to miss the words. She sighed before speaking again. "But for the wedding, she'd want whatever her mum would want, and that means getting as close to the original as possible."

"Yes, but if we got her these, it'd be the perfect excuse not to tell Sarah what happened to the original ones. We could just say they were a treat, and you know full well your sister won't say no to Evie."

CHAPTER TEN

"I can't believe how little this place has changed," Maggie said, looking around the café as she pushed the bags of shopping into the corner. She wasn't sure about the pair of jeans Nathan had persuaded her to buy, but just knowing what was in the small shoebox gave her a glow she hadn't had for a long time. It was ridiculous that a pair of shoes that weren't even for her could do that, but she couldn't wait to give them to her niece.

She hadn't been in this café since she'd moved to London. Her short trips home had been about spending time with her family and the Parkers — well, some of them — so she hadn't even considered coming into town. Floral pelmets and curtains still framed the café's lead-panelled windows, although the fabric was newer than the stuff she remembered. The twinkle of fairy lights in the window and a small tree that perched on a shelf in the furthest corner were the only acknowledgement of Christmas, although the place was so crammed with tables that anything more would probably be a fire hazard.

"Well, if it isn't Maggie Green," a familiar voice said as she settled into a plush chair.

Maggie looked up to see Mrs Watkins, her customary blue rinse firmly in place, curls tight against her scalp. The welcoming smile was also unchanged.

"I wondered if we'd see you with the wedding coming up."

"Mrs Watkins, how lovely to see you."

"And you, dear. It must be years since you and young Nathan were in here together. Do you remember that time you spilled your milkshake on that tourist? She went completely mad. I reckon she must have lost her marbles long before that happened. She hadn't stopped moaning about one thing or another from the moment she stepped in here."

Mrs Watkins didn't pause for breath as she continued with the story. Maggie swapped a knowing glance with Nathan. She wasn't about to admit that the incident had been anything but an accident. She could still remember the nasty way the woman had spoken to the waitress Mrs Watkins had employed that summer. The poor girl had fled to the kitchen in tears, and the woman hadn't been much nicer to Mrs Watkins. A bit of milkshake down her polyester dress was the least she'd deserved. Mrs Watkins's ramble through her memories of the things that had happened over the years made Maggie smile, and she smiled at Nathan, sharing her amusement with him. Living on the outskirts of a tiny village meant neither of them had ever passed up the opportunity to come into town if someone was driving in. Unfortunately, it was only a small town, and Mrs Watkins had been one of the few business owners who had been happy to have a couple of youngsters hanging around when they didn't have much money to spend, although they'd always shown up with just enough money for one of her amazing homemade milkshakes or hot chocolates. The sort of thing that would cost you the best part of a tenner in London these days used to cost them less than a pound here. Mrs Watkins had always given them a sticky bun, or a cream cake, for free. When they had protested, she'd always insisted that she'd only have to throw them out if they didn't eat them.

Nathan smiled back at Maggie, reaching his hand out to take hers, squeezing it with a wink. A shiver travelled through her, the sensation of his warm strong hand on hers blocking out Mrs Watkins's words. She could only focus on the feel of his palm against the back of her hand. His callouses against her own soft skin threatened to overwhelm her. Her eyes dropped to take in his large hand covering her own. The sight sent a wave of longing through her that she hadn't felt in a long time.

"Ah, it's about time you two got together," Mrs Watkins said, glancing down at the joined hands before looking back up at them both, a beaming smile on her face.

Maggie felt her jaw drop at the assumption, and she pulled her hand free from Nathan's. Placing her hands in her lap, she tried to ignore the sense of loss.

"You two were always made for each other. It warms my heart to see that you've finally realised it as well. Anyway, what would you like to drink?" Mrs Watkins continued before Maggie could form a sentence. The quick change in subject had thrown her, almost as much as the realisation people thought she and Nathan should be a couple.

"Sorry?"

"I've got the gingerbread hot chocolate, or would you prefer chocolate milkshake? I seem to remember those were your favourites."

"Gingerbread hot chocolate, please," Maggie replied, deciding to ignore everything else. It was very definitely shaping up to be a chocolate day, and the gingerbread hot chocolate was her all-time favourite. Despite trying just about every version she could find in the city, she'd never been able to find one as good as Mrs Watkins's.

"Coming right up," Mrs Watkins said, after taking Nathan's order for the same drink.

"While we have a minute to ourselves, I need to talk to you about something," Nathan said.

Oh God, what now? Please don't let it be about what Mrs Watkins just said. Actually, please don't let it be about that night, Maggie thought. She couldn't bear the humiliation of being forced to talk to him about that. In the face of her silence, he carried on.

"I wanted to apologise about the barn."

Oh, the barn. She wasn't sure that was any better as a subject, but she could probably cope. "Why?"

"It was our dream. We talked about it our whole childhoods and I bought it on my own."

Maggie took a breath. The fact she wasn't a part of that hurt more than it should have, maybe because it would be a solid, permanent, reminder that they wouldn't be a part of each other's lives in the way they had planned. In the way she had hoped.

"You don't need to apologise to me," she said. "As you've said, it is the perfect place for you to live and have your business."

"I know, and I couldn't pass it up, but it feels weird being there without you. It must feel weird to you that I'm there."

"I never imagined either of us would live there alone, but let's be honest, we were kids when we made all those plans. We're adults now, we know you can't live with your best friend forever. If nothing else we'd both have got married one day, and I can't imagine our husband or wife being happy living all together." Maggie forced a jokey tone and changed the subject.

It wasn't something she'd thought about for a long time, but the idea of Nathan getting married made everything inside her squeeze painfully. She shoved the thought away. Thank goodness she'd ordered the hot chocolate. There was no way she was going to get through the rest of this day without chocolate, and lots of it.

Heading back to the car, Maggie lifted the collar of her coat around her neck and hunched into it, trying to keep the icy air that swirled down the funnel of the high street from creeping inside her layers. The intensity of the cold made her glad Nathan had talked her into buying the jeans. Her skirt and tights might look elegant with her boots, but they were doing nothing to protect her from the chill.

Realising she couldn't hear Nathan's footsteps beside her anymore, Maggie stopped to see him a few paces behind her, peering at the pub.

"That's Paula," he said, gesturing to the window. "Let's go say hi."

As they walked into the pub, the heat hit instantly, wrapping around her like a blanket. Christmas tunes provided a steady background noise to the almost empty bar. The place was smaller than Maggie remembered, but now it had the feel of any chain pub anywhere in the country. Looking around, she spotted a familiar logo on the curled menus placed on every table, reinforcing that it wasn't the independent pub of their youth anymore. She was surprised it was worthwhile for the brewery to come somewhere as remote as this. Even McDonald's hadn't made it here.

"Hi, Paula, are you okay?" Nathan asked, standing next to the window table Paula was occupying.

"I'm good, just waiting for Chris. We came into town to stock up on a few more baby bits," she said as she patted her round stomach with a smile.

"Let me guess, someone roped him in to help with an emergency."

"Got it in one. The surgery have a leak," Paula smiled. "I'm okay, though. I have my book, and I certainly won't get hungry or thirsty while I wait."

"Why don't we give you a lift home? We're on our way now," Nathan suggested, turning back to Paula.

"That would be great, if you don't mind. It's lovely and warm in here, but I don't know how many more Christmas songs I can take." Paula gave a good-natured grimace towards the speaker stuck on the wall in the corner.

As Nathan steered his truck down a country lane, Maggie twisted so she could speak to Paula, who was sitting in the back. She'd insisted on sitting there so she could sprawl out — something she'd said was a real necessity the bigger she got.

"When is the baby due?"

"Middle of January," Paula replied, gently stroking her stomach with a smile. "To be honest, it can't be soon enough now. I'm sure I can't get much bigger without popping."

"You look really well," Maggie said with a smile.

"It's snowing," Nathan exclaimed, his tone filled with joy, drawing Maggie's attention to the windscreen which indeed dotting with snowflakes.

"You still love snow, then?" she asked, resisting the urge to tease him for pointing out the obvious.

"What's not to love? It's brilliant," he said. Despite the falling light of the day, his smile was unmissable.

"Well, with the amount of time you spent in hot countries, we could be forgiven for thinking you don't like the cold!" Paula laughed.

"Maybe I really missed it," Nathan laughed back.

"Maybe the lure of all those bikini clad women was stronger than your love of snow," Paula countered.

"Don't know what you mean," he replied with a lofty tone.

"You know exactly what I mean. I've seen all the photos. The question is, when are you going to settle down?"

"Paula," Nathan said, his playful tone vanishing.

Maggie could feel his body tense next to her own, but Paula just laughed again.

"That tone might work on other people, Nathan Parker, but I know you too well. Come on, exactly how many girlfriends do you have at the moment? You need to fall in love."

Maggie stilled. Girlfriends, as in plural? When Dean told her Nathan wasn't bringing anyone to the wedding, she had assumed he was single, not that he had so many he wouldn't be able to pick one.

"I don't have one girlfriend, Paula. Never mind multiple ones," Nathan replied with a sigh.

"All right then, if you say so," Paula laughed. "In need of a rest after years of juggling women, then?"

"You spend too much time listening to my brothers," Nathan said. "I have never *juggled* women. They seem to think that I've been involved with any woman I know on social media, or who's in the same photo."

"So you didn't fall in love, then?" Paula asked hopefully.

Maggie sucked in a breath at the question, torn between wanting to know and wanting to get as far away from the conversation as possible. She wasn't sure she could take the answer.

Nathan was silent for so long Maggie began to think he wouldn't answer, and while she knew it would be for the best if he didn't, a part of her was screaming at him to just answer the question.

Finally, still staring straight ahead, he spoke quietly. "I gave my heart away a long time ago, and I never got it back."

Maggie felt the breath whoosh out of her as a band tightened around her chest. Well, now she knew. That's what you got for being curious.

"She must have been some woman to keep your attention," Paula said with a smile.

Nathan didn't reply but gave Paula a wry smile via the rear-view mirror. Maggie swallowed hard on the disappointment that climbed up her throat.

Loosening the seatbelt where it had tightened around her stomach, Maggie watched Paula lean on Nathan as they made their way along the slabbed footpath to the house she and Chris had bought a couple of years earlier. Taking the keys from Paula, he unlocked the door and walked her in. Maggie turned her gaze away from the door and up to the sky that was now a blanket of unrelenting white.

The street was beginning to resemble a Christmas card, with only the tracks of the few cars that had been passing marring the perfection. Watching his tenderness with his pregnant sister-in-law was too much of a reminder of the Nathan Maggie had grown up with. From when they had been really young he had always put himself out for others. They had both been six, busy chasing around after Nathan's big brothers, when she'd broken her leg. It had been her first broken bone, but a long way from being her last. They had all been swinging across the river on a rope bridge Dean had rigged up. The boys had said Maggie was too little to go on it, but she had been determined and, as soon as Dean had turned his back, she'd grabbed the rope and gone for it. Unfortunately, Dean had been right. Maggie hadn't had enough strength to hang on and had fallen just short of the safety on the other side, breaking her leg in the process.

All that summer Nathan had stayed with her, making up stories and playing games. They had hidden in a den Maggie's mum had made and thrown mud pies at the other Parker boys whenever they passed. The memory of her mother tightened her chest. She'd had enough of missing people, but how did you let the people you cared about into your life when you knew they were going to leave in the end? She was smart enough to know that relationships were often different to the one you hoped for, but she didn't know how to deal with the fact they would always end. Maybe that was why she'd dated Rupert. The fact they'd worked together meant things had run smoothly between them, but maybe it had been as much about the fact she hadn't cared for him as deeply as she was supposed to care for a boyfriend? Had she chosen him to protect her heart? The fact she was more upset about her job than losing him was probably all the answer she needed.

Pulling up outside his parents' place, Nathan put the handbrake on and heaved a sigh of relief. He would certainly be staying here tonight. The snow had been unrelenting, and he'd got Maggie back safely but it was going to be far too treacherous to consider going back out. He'd call Paula later and make sure that she was okay, in case Chris hadn't made it home.

He couldn't see anyone, but the sound of shrieking and laughter reached them inside the truck.

"Sounds like a snowball fight," Nathan said, turning to Maggie.

She'd been worryingly silent since Paula had started quizzing him about his love life. Nathan loved his sister-in-law dearly, but he could have happily throttled her when she started up in front of Maggie.

Maggie cocked her head to listen, before turning her head to smile at him, a smile so brilliant that it took his breath away. "Shall we go join them?" she asked, her eyes bright.

71

"Oh yes," he said, feeling how broad the smile on his own face was. That, just that reaction, that glimmer of mischief in her chocolate eyes, that was the Maggie he knew.

"It looks like those jeans you insisted I buy are going to come in handy sooner than I thought," she said.

"Good idea, do you want me to let you into the house to change?"

"No, if I go into the warmth I won't want to come out again," Maggie replied with a grin. "Give me a moment, I'll do it here."

She climbed into the back of the truck, and Nathan kept his eyes forward to give her the privacy to change. The thought of her slipping that skirt down her pale thighs sent a flash of heat through him.

"I still can't believe you didn't own a single pair of jeans," he said, needing to stop his thoughts from being able to roam free. The realisation that she'd worn those fancy trousers to the park yesterday because she didn't own anything casual had been a shock. The Maggie he knew had lived in jeans — well, those or princess dresses.

"I haven't worn jeans for years," she said, the broken way the words came out making it clear she was contorting herself in the small space to pull the denim on. Nathan swallowed hard, wondering what it would feel like to ease his hands up her legs, the way the jeans were doing right now.

"Just as well you bought those, then. You'd be frozen in five minutes in those corporate outfits you live in at the moment," he said, trying very hard not to think about his brother's girlfriend being half naked in his truck.

Maggie climbed out and Nathan took a beat to enjoy the way she filled out the jeans before frowning at the sight of those shiny red boots. They made her legs look spectacular, but the heels and array of holes up the sides meant they weren't suited to playing in the snow, not safely anyway.

"Let's get you some wellies before we start," he said, gesturing to the house. "You can borrow a pair of Mum's."

Heading to the front door, he grabbed a small pair from the mountain of boots and shoes that were always piled there, and let Maggie use his shoulder to balance as she pulled her own boots off and slid her feet into the wellies.

"Same tactics?" she said, her smile so bright he could believe she'd catapulted them back through time to when their friendship had been unmarred.

He nodded his agreement. It might have been years, but the pair of them were a formidable force when it came to snowball fights.

The chances of anyone hearing them from the back garden, with the racket that was coming from there, were slim but the pair of them moved quietly. Looking to all the world like they thought they were in a Bond film, they hunched over and crept towards the side of the house, the snow crunching lightly with every step. Without saying a word, they both stopped just before the back gate, and with a thumbs up began to build a mound of snowballs, piling them onto the recycling box lid.

Once they had a decent stash, they grabbed the lid and eased the gate open. The creak of old hinges gave them away instantly, and before they could get through the space, a volley of snow bombarded them. Maggie shrieked, pulling Nathan in front of her like a human shield, and he laughed, the sheer pleasure of playing together filling that empty space inside of him, at least for now.

CHAPTER ELEVEN

Stretched out on the clinical bed, Maggie looked longingly at the skirt and knickers folded neatly on the chair beside her. The fragile blue paper towel covering her most intimate parts didn't feel like anywhere near enough. Her consultant was pleasant enough, but she didn't imagine there was a woman alive who would face having a near stranger peering into her bits with anything other than rolling dread. She wished she could magic herself away, back to her day with Nathan. Laid out here, the fun she'd had reconnecting with her friend seemed like a lifetime away, not a couple of days.

"Ready, Miss Green?" the nurse asked, her smiling face appearing around the curtain that had been pulled, dividing the consultation room in half. As though not having the consultant or nurse watch her take the bottom half of her clothing off and get onto the bed would make the experience less mortifying.

Maggie had always been a good girl, going for all her medical checks whenever they were due, regardless of how unpleasant they might be, but that didn't mean she enjoyed them. She forced a smile at the nurse and nodded. The nurse's face disappeared just long enough for her to have indicated to Dr Brooks that he could start.

"Okay, Miss Green, just relax. As we've discussed, this may take a few minutes, but we'll make sure we complete the tests today."

Relax? Seriously? Only a man would say something as stupid as that when he was about to start shoving cold metal into someone's body. Maggie resisted the urge to snap, instead just nodding.

Just breathe, the voice in her head advised. She focused on pulling air into her lungs in a steady flow. Ignoring the man with what was essentially a giant pair of binoculars between her thighs was easier said than done. *Just breathe*, she reminded herself. In, out. Biting down on her thumb, she tried to ignore the sensation. It wasn't painful, not really, but it was damned uncomfortable having someone poking and prodding away down there.

"Thank you, Miss Green. If you'd like to put your clothes back on, we can discuss the next steps," Dr Brooks said, as he snapped his rubber gloves off.

Having pulled her skirt and underwear back on, Maggie slipped her feet into her heels. She forced herself to step out from behind the modesty curtain and take the seat next to the consultant. He scribbled away at his notes for a few beats, the scratching of his expensive gold pen the only sound in the small room. She resisted the urge to slap the pen out of his hand, placing her hands primly on her lap instead. Just when she despaired of him ever talking to her, he carefully placed the cap back onto his pen and turned to face her.

"Obviously we will have to wait for the lab results for a definitive picture, but there are visible abnormalities in the cells of your cervix."

Maggie swallowed, not allowing her mind to wander to the terrifying possibility that presented itself. She was calm, collected and rational; she could handle a conversation. "What does that mean?"

"As you know, we undertake the colposcopy to identify areas of abnormality and take biopsies of those areas. That biopsy enables us to determine the nature of the abnormality, and whether any further treatment is required."

"So you can't tell me anything until the results come back?"

"We can't give you a definitive answer. However, I can tell you that your area of abnormality is extensive, and as such we would recommend a minor procedure to remove that area, regardless of the results of the biopsy."

Minor. Her mind hung on to the word. Minor was good, right?

"So you can't tell what it is yet?"

"We can't be certain at this stage."

Maggie paused; there was something about his phrasing that caught her attention. "You can't be certain, but you do this a lot; what do you think it is?"

"I don't like to speculate, Miss Green."

"I appreciate that, but if you were certain it was a benign abnormality, would you tell me?"

"Yes, if I believed that was the case I would say."

"So you think it could be…" Maggie paused, stumbling over the word. She'd thought it enough over the last few days, but somehow found that saying it out loud was terrifying on a whole new level. "Cancer." She rubbed her suddenly damp palms on her skirt, trying to ignore the slimy sensation that wound through her.

"I'm sorry, Miss Green; given the extent and nature of the abnormality, I believe that cancer remains a possible outcome."

The room spun as the voice in Maggie's head reminded her to breathe. Drawing a deep breath in she fought to release it, nodding, as though trying to reassure Dr Brooks that she wasn't about to fall apart completely.

"So, what happens next?" she asked, when she could trust herself to speak again.

The next few minutes passed in a blur of medical information and advice. Maggie nodded, trying desperately to take it all in as her brain glitched, flickering and losing any sense of what Dr Brooks was explaining to her every time he said the word cancer. Before she knew it, she was walking out of the sprawling hospital, leaflets clutched in her hand, her appointment for the next week arranged, and her entire life changed.

CHAPTER TWELVE

Vaulting over the stile, Nathan landed hard on the other side, barely breaking his stride before he set off across the field. The beat of Imagine Dragons' latest album kept his pace up even as he fought through the familiar pain that always hit in the first ten minutes of his run. He knew once he came out of the other side of it, the sheer joy of the exertion would take over, but damn, it never got any easier. The snow that had looked so beautiful for the last few days was turning into the kind of grey slush that he knew was going to saturate his trainers within minutes, but he needed to be outside, he needed to try to clear his head.

Running along the public right of way that the neighbouring farmer kept clear and passable, he silently forced his thoughts away from Maggie, yet every time he tried, his mind slipped back to the mischievous look on her face when she'd been throwing snowballs. It was as though his brain couldn't process anything that wasn't her. Hitting the volume on his phone, he ratcheted the sound up, determined to block out his own thoughts.

Leaving the field and hitting the road that would loop him around the outskirts of the village, he paused to let a car pass before setting off. Pacing himself to the beat of the next track, he kept moving, cursing as his mind wandered despite the pulse of music. He paused the music at the sound of an engine. His gear was hi-viz, but that didn't help much on a single-track road that twisted around multiple sharp bends. Turning, he moved to the side of the road and tucked himself into the hedgerow, ignoring the scrape of branches poking through the thin fabric of his running gear. Raising his hand in greeting as the car passed, he shifted and set off again.

His mind filled with thoughts of Maggie again. They'd had such a good time in town together, and when they'd arrived back and she'd leapt into the snowball fight, it had been as though no time had passed at all. Unfortunately, as soon as the cold had sunk into their bones, she'd vanished back to the Green house, and he hadn't seen her since. He really wanted to believe she wasn't avoiding him, but he knew it was naïve to think one fun afternoon would be enough to fix everything.

As he hit the centre of the village his phone rang, and taking the opportunity to catch his breath and distract himself, he stopped to answer the call, despite the unknown number flashing on the screen.

"Hello."

"Hello, is that Nathan Parker?" a smooth, cultured voice asked.

"Yes."

"My name is Charlie. I am calling on behalf of Andersson Hotels."

Nathan frowned; he knew of the Andersson Hotels as one of the world's most exclusive hotel brands; he doubted there was anyone who didn't. What he didn't understand was why they were calling him. He'd never been able to afford to stay in one, so it wasn't as if he could have left something behind, or not paid a bill.

"How can I help you, Charlie?"

"Clarissa Andersson has come across some of your bespoke furniture and has asked me to try and arrange a meeting with you."

Nathan somehow made it through the conversation without sounding as shell-shocked as he felt. The idea of his furniture gracing the Andersson's rooms left him lightheaded. Okay, so there was no guarantee the meeting would lead to anything, but to have caught the eye of such a discerning brand, wow. He sucked in a breath, and leaning against the dusty stone wall of the cottage he'd paused next to, he bent forward, inhaling deeply. A commission like that would change his life. He'd never be short of work again. He could afford to finish the barn in the foreseeable future, instead of it being a distant hope.

Pulling himself upright, he allowed a wide grin to spread across his face. He had a lot of work to do if he was going to have enough to present them with on Christmas Eve. Suddenly aware of the chill seeping into him from the cold stone, he pushed away from the wall and set off again at full pace, his head suddenly full of designs he needed to sketch out.

CHAPTER THIRTEEN

Maggie hadn't been able to face heading home, instead walking around Bristol in a blur, watching people shopping, some hurtling around as though determined to fit two days of activity into one, others meandering. Somehow, the world had continued to turn. She knew she couldn't face Sarah until she had a handle on her emotions, especially given the fact that she had deliberately hidden the appointment from her sister.

Once she was back in Honeyford, she delayed further by visiting the churchyard. Ignoring the cold and damp that seeped through the thin fabric of her tights almost instantly, Maggie knelt in front of her parents' grave. She carefully picked up the errant petals and leaves that were scattered across the mature grass. Anything to avoid looking at the headstone. The words on it were etched into her mind as permanently as they were carved into the stone.

Maggie had wanted to visit before — the guilt that she hadn't had been building up — but she hadn't been able to do it until now. Today, though, she just needed to be somewhere where no one had any expectations of her. She'd made it here, but she wasn't quite ready to face it yet, so she busied herself tidying up. She wished she could find solace in visiting. Over the years she had watched people in the cemetery either chatter away to their loved ones, or sit in silence as if keeping them company. She'd never been able to find that sense of peace from her visits. Instead, she felt exhausted after visiting, as if being here meant facing the worst of herself.

Pulling the dead flowers from the vase, she put them to one side with her collection of leaves and petals. She'd take them to the bin on her way out. The crinkle of cellophane seemed to echo into the silence as she carefully unwrapped the giant daisies and roses she had brought with her. Holding them to her nose, she pulled in a deep breath. The scent was so familiar that, even after all these years, she could almost believe she was running into the house after school. Her Mary Janes clicking on the parquet floor, as she passed the permanently full vase on the hallway table, on her way into the kitchen to hug her mum before snagging a freshly baked cookie. She could almost believe she was crawling around the floor, pushing her Barbie campervan around as her dad arrived home from work, a bunch of flowers in one hand, the other sliding around her mum's back as he pulled his wife in for a kiss.

But she wasn't there, she was here, kneeling next to their grave, the only light coming from the candle-filled lanterns that flickered on the surrounding graves. She placed the flowers in the vase and she sat back on her heels to inspect her handiwork. If Sarah had done it, they would be so perfectly arranged that they wouldn't look out of place in a magazine, but that was the advantage of her sister having worked as a florist for a few months. Her own efforts were a bit shabby in comparison, but she had tried.

Maggie finally looked up at the headstone. The words *forever in their hearts* were carved below both her and Sarah's names. It wasn't enough; she didn't want them forever in her heart. She wanted them here, in her life. She needed her parents, needed the guidance they would give. The thought sent a lurch of guilt through her and she rubbed her temple, blinking back the tears that welled in her eyes. She had Sarah. Her sister had dropped out of university and given up her own dreams to raise Maggie — what was wrong that it wasn't enough? The responsibility she felt whenever she thought of her sister was overwhelming.

The need to repay Sarah for her sacrifice drove her every action. People were always telling Maggie how successful she was, how proud they were of her. Didn't anyone realise it wasn't her? It was the burning need to make sure that Sarah never had to worry about money. It wasn't enough, but it was the only thing Maggie could do. Maybe if she sent enough money to Sarah, she would be good enough. Maybe Sarah wouldn't leave her, just like everyone else did.

"How could you leave me?" she whispered to her parents, the tears finally spilling over, tracing their way down her cheeks.

What kind of person was she that she resented them for leaving her? But she did; they had left her, everyone left her, and now she might be the one leaving the few people she had left. She sucked a breath in, fighting the nausea the flowed through her.

Shifting on her heels, she leant forward and traced the words with her finger.

"Are you okay?"

Maggie swung her head around to see Nathan standing behind her in running gear, a look of concern on his face. She rubbed her face, trying to dry the tears that refused to stop flowing as she rose. Her joints were stiff from kneeling on the ground for so long, making her movements awkward. As she wobbled on her heels, Nathan reached out, holding her elbow to stabilise her. The action was so reminiscent of him doing the same thing when they had stood here together at the funeral that she froze. The heat that the contact sent through her wasn't the same, though. She reluctantly looked up at him. In his ratty jogging pants and hoodie he looked so different from the suited and booted men she was used to spending her time with, but he seemed so much more real.

Reaching out with his other hand, Nathan gently held her other arm, the movement bringing him closer to her. Maggie just stared up at him. Her emotions were so raw, everything was so close to the surface that she couldn't speak. She couldn't find the strength to bring her walls back up. She wanted the comfort being with him had given her when they were best friends, back before she had humiliated herself and ruined everything. She looked away, unable to take the intensity in his gaze, and trying really hard not to care that he had caught her in such a mess, but when he pulled her to him, wrapping his arms around her, she simply leant in and let herself enjoy the feeling of being held, the heat from his chest warming her and chasing away the chill that seemed to have seeped into her bones.

"Just breathe," Nathan said quietly, his hand stroking up and down her back, and she obeyed the familiar words. The voice was the same one that spoke to her in all the tough moments of her life, now outside of her head for the first time in years, its familiarity unravelling her control.

Nathan just stood, silently holding her, and her tears began to flow again, for the parents she would never get to know as people, for the life she had missed out on, for the love she had lost, for the fear she would die before she could find a way to be good enough for anyone to stick around. The fact it was that lost love, the man who had left her, comforting her, seemed irrelevant in that moment. Maggie simply let herself feel, sinking into her own fears. In the flickering light, she cried for everything she had lost and for everything she could never have.

CHAPTER FOURTEEN

Nathan stood, holding Maggie in his arms, his heart breaking at the feel of her body shuddering against his. When he'd spotted her in the graveyard, he'd run over, bursting to tell her his good news. Yet as he'd come closer, he'd slowed, knowing something wasn't right.

He'd never been able to cope with Maggie's tears. They reminded him that he'd always been helpless to make things better for her. Tightening his arms around the woman he'd been desperate to hold from the moment he'd seen her again just a couple of weeks ago, he blinked against the moisture in his own eyes.

When stood here together fifteen years ago, Maggie had been dry-eyed, the pair of them watching the men who lowered her parents' coffins into the ground. It had been a sunny day and the drab black of everyone's clothes had seemed to suck in the light. He had stood at Maggie's side, staring at the hedge on the side of the graveyard, watching the small leaves flutter in the gentle breeze rather than looking at the coffins as they were lowered into the ground. He had held Maggie's hand, refusing to let go, even when her great aunt, only able to attend because a carer from her old people's home was pushing her withered body around in a wheelchair, had tried to take his place at her side. He hadn't been able to understand how all those old people had been there when Maggie's parents weren't.

Nathan remembered thinking that the adults had been being really weird that day. They'd all spoken to Maggie in really quiet voices, telling her it was okay to cry. He hadn't understood it then. Why had they kept telling her that? It wasn't like she hadn't known it. She was already sad; as far as he was concerned, she didn't need reminding. Now he understood their worry over the silence from the normally boisterous Maggie; they'd needed the reassurance of her grief to know she was going to be okay.

Holding her in the graveyard now, he felt the heat of her tears as they saturated his sweatshirt, but he didn't relax his hold. Instead, desperate to find a way to take the pain away for her, he continued to gently rub one hand up and down her back.

Sarah had sobbed throughout the funeral. Nathan had known he was supposed to be worried about her as well, but he could only remember his relief that she'd decided to give up university to live with Maggie. Only eleven, he hadn't considered that Maggie could end up living somewhere else, somewhere he wouldn't be able to see her, but the shock of that realisation had been like a tidal wave that had washed away anything other than the pure relief that it wasn't going to happen.

"Want to go to the barn after this?" he had whispered, determined to help her escape from the weird way everyone was looking at her. When they had been alone in the barn she had finally cried. The forgotten memory was shaken loose by standing here with her again. How had he forgotten that moment? He had just lain on the dusty floor next to Maggie, holding her hand in his. The terror at being unable to take her sadness away was still as clear in his mind now as it had been all those years ago. He could still feel the sensation of their sweaty palms, pressed together in the heat, but he hadn't minded that any more than he minded the wetness that was saturating his top now. He had just wanted to be with her.

Just like he did now. How had it taken him so long to realise just how important she was to him?

"I won't leave you," he whispered, the words the same ones he had said to her all those years ago. This time he really understood the promise he was making as it slipped from his lips.

Maggie pulled back as he spoke, and he instantly felt the loss of her warmth against him. Her pale, tear-streaked face looked up at him in shock as he whispered his promise. She blinked, her bright eyes wide, and he knew she too was remembering him saying those words to her on that awful day. Something hopeful and heated flared in her expression and he reached for her, determined to hold her in his arms again, but her jaw tightened and, as though a mask had fallen into place, she shook her head before backing away from him.

CHAPTER FIFTEEN

Ignoring the missed call from the company, Maggie quickly cleared the screen and brought up the camera app on her phone. She hadn't bothered listening to any of the voicemails since the first one. How many times did they need to ask her to return her security card? It wasn't like they weren't aware she was going to be away from home for a few weeks, so they knew exactly why she hadn't done it yet.

"Smile," she said to Evie, wanting to capture a picture of her niece, who was manning the 'guess the number of sweets in the jar' stall.

The tradition of the eldest students each taking a turn to man some of the stalls at the school Christmas fete was one that had carried on since she and Nathan had been at school.

"How long until you finish your shift?" she asked Evie as she forwarded the photo to Dean, knowing her niece was desperate to be free to go and spend the money Sarah and Paul had given her on the array of stalls that filled the assembly hall.

"Ten minutes," Evie replied.

"Okay, I'm going to get a drink. If you want to leave the hall, come and find me first," Maggie said.

"I'm allowed to go around the school, you know," Evie said with a frown.

"I know, but your mum is busy helping with the tombola so I just want to make sure I know where you are."

Evie rolled her eyes but nodded her agreement.

Once she'd braved the queue for a paper cup of hot chocolate, Maggie scanned the crowded room, looking for a spare chair. The only one she could see was at a table crammed into the corner. Tess from the bakery and Susie sat at it. Oh well, she wasn't about to stand up for the next hour or so because Susie was being weird.

"Mind if I join you?" Maggie asked, smiling at the two women.

"Of course not," Tess said, half standing to wrap one arm around Maggie in greeting. "How are you?"

"I'm good, although I think I'm going to have a headache after this," Maggie said with a smile. "I don't know how Sarah is coping; she came hours ago to help with the set up, and she's going to be here to help clear up. You wouldn't know she's getting married tomorrow."

"She's bonkers. I'm only here until I can drag Finn away," Tess said, gesturing to her son, who was standing with his friend and seemed to have spilled something very purple down his white jumper.

"Good luck with that; he looks like he's in for the duration," Maggie said with a laugh as the crowds shifted and Finn disappeared along with his friend. Well, at least one person was pleased to see her, she thought, as she gave Tess a quick hug in return, trying to ignore the less than friendly response from Susie, who was avoiding looking at her.

As she was stripping off her coat and scarf, her phone vibrated in her skirt pocket and she pulled it out.

"What's put that smile on your face?" Tess asked.

"Dean. I sent him a photo of Evie at her stall, and he's reminded me of the Christmas we all tried to replace the star on the top of the tree in this hall with a fake poo from the joke shop in town."

Maggie turned to Susie, trying to draw her into the shared memory, but if anything, the woman's face was even more of a scowl. Maggie smoothed her skirt self-consciously; she'd dressed in a skirt and blouse combination that paired with the cutaway heels she loved, and normally gave her confidence a real boost, but as Susie gave her a dismissive look up and down, she felt out of place.

"You've left off the best bit of that story." Nathan's voice broke into their discussion, and she had to strain her neck to look at him where he stood, hands resting on the back of the chair, that half smile in place as he met her gaze.

"You've forgotten to mention the bit where you overbalanced and took the whole tree down, landing it on me, Dean and Susie, and taking away any chance of the school not knowing it was us," Nathan said, his smile growing.

"Oh God, don't remind me," Susie said, covering her burning face with her hands. "We all got into so much trouble, and it took my mum ages to forgive me."

"Totally worth it, though, to see old Mrs Barker's face when she realised what we'd been up to."

"It didn't help that the fake poo had landed right near the door," Susie said. "It took twenty minutes for her to calm down enough to listen to us explain that it wasn't actually a real one."

The three of them started laughing together, and for a brief moment, Maggie remembered exactly how much she loved these people and realised just how much she'd missed them.

"Come on, let's go spend a fortune on tat and eat a month's worth of sugar," Nathan said, grabbing Maggie's hand and helping her to her feet.

Maggie let herself be pulled in Nathan's wake, smiling at the familiar and not so familiar faces as he made his way through the crowds.

Moving from one classroom to the next, the pair of them were handing money over faster than she would have thought possible, thanks to Nathan insisting that they have a go at everything.

"I didn't think I'd be back here, trying to throw a bean bag into Santa's chimney," Maggie said.

"I'm just surprised you're still as terrible at it as you were when this was our school," Nathan said, laughing as yet another of her efforts went skidding straight past the target.

"So hand-eye co-ordination isn't one of my strengths, you love me anyway," she said with a laugh, her brow furrowed as she concentrated on her next throw.

When her last one missed, she sighed.

"Okay, I admit defeat; there is no way I can do that, it's just too hard." Maggie turned to Nathan, expecting to share a smile at the sight of a girl who couldn't be more than about eight, throwing bean bags into the chimney with total ease.

Instead, Nathan was staring at her, his expression blank, as though he was in a completely different world.

"Are you okay?" she asked.

Nathan blinked, as though pulling himself back to the present, before giving her a smile that didn't quite reach his eyes and nodding. "Let's go and see if we can win a bottle," he said, dragging her in the direction of the library, which had been the home of the Christmas fete tombola for as long as either of them could remember.

"I can't believe it," Maggie said, laughing with her sister and nodding to the bottle as Sarah handed it over. "I never win, and when I do it has to be something like that."

"Come on, I know for a fact you've drunk Lambrini before," Nathan said.

"Not in the last decade, I haven't," Maggie said. "If I'm going to drink wine, I don't want it to be sweeter than a bag of candy, and I want it to have enough alcohol to take the edge off, not so weak I'd drown my insides before I got tipsy."

She grabbed her phone out, snapping a picture and adding the caption, *I'm saving my prize for you*, before sending it to Dean.

He replied almost instantly with a green-faced emoji and the comment, *if you're planning to share prizes with me, I'd rather wait for your lottery win*.

Giggling, she showed the screen to Sarah and Nathan.

"He'll have a long wait; you don't even do the lottery," Sarah said with a laugh, but Nathan just frowned.

"Come on, it's your turn, Nathan," Sarah said, pulling a smile from him.

When Nathan had failed to win anything other than a bottle of bubble bath, something they all found hilarious, given the fact he didn't have a bath in the barn, they left Sarah to deal with the next influx of visitors to the tombola stand, and moved on to the next classroom.

Nathan's good humour returned in full force at finding the football challenge in the year two classroom.

"Do you remember us running this in our last year here?" Nathan asked.

Maggie nodded; she'd wanted to run a different stall, she couldn't even remember which one now, but Nathan had persuaded her that they needed to do the football challenge together. He'd loved playing goalie for the half hour the pair of them had run the stall, leaving her to take the money from the endless queue of kids waiting for their turn.

"It's as popular as ever," Maggie said, as they took their place in line.

When they finally made it to the front of the queue, Nathan asked the boy standing in goal if he could swap with him while Maggie took her shots.

"Do you really need to embarrass me again?" she asked, smiling at the memory of trying to get a shot past him. Despite having unlimited free goes before the fete had started, she hadn't managed it once.

Nathan shook his shoulders loose, giving her that half smile she'd always loved. "Give me your best shot."

Squaring her own shoulders, Maggie slipped her shoes off and forced her gaze to the bottom left corner of the net that took up the best part of one wall of the classroom, before taking the short run up and kicking the ball as hard as she could towards the opposite side of the goal.

Nathan was already moving to his right before he realised what she'd done, and as the ball connected with the net Maggie threw her arms up.

"Yes, she shoots, she scores," she crowed, unable to stop her laughter from bubbling over.

"What?" Nathan exclaimed. "How the hell did you pull that off?"

"Sheer skill," Maggie laughed, knowing skill had about as much to do with her lucky shot as the football-themed activity had to do with Christmas.

"No way, I demand a replay," he said.

"No chance," Maggie said, accepting her prize, a yellow lollipop, and sticking her tongue out at Nathan before sticking the lolly in her mouth. "I won, fair and square."

"Fine," Nathan said, mock annoyance colouring his voice.

She gave him a wink.

"It's good to see you having fun," Nathan said, slinging his arm over her shoulder as he led her out of the classroom, in search of the next activity to try.

At his words, Maggie realised she was, and that she couldn't remember the last time she'd enjoyed herself so much. She certainly wouldn't have dreamed of bringing Rupert to a school Christmas fete. If she'd really had to force him to a Christmas-themed event, she might have got away with the food festival at the Olympia, maybe, but never something as simple, but joyful, as this.

CHAPTER SIXTEEN

"It's wonderful having you home," Sarah said, her eyes filling again.

"Don't start crying again. I don't know how many times you can redo your make-up in one day," Maggie said with a smile, passing her sister another tissue from the box she'd kept on hand all morning. She smiled brightly to try to push back the moisture that filled her own eyes.

"I mean it. I've missed you." Sarah pulled her in for a hug and Evie crossed the room, wrapping her spindly arms around both of their waists.

"Me too, Auntie Maggie," she said.

"I missed you guys too, but I will have to go back to work." Maggie swallowed hard on the words, feeling as though she was lying, but she really would need to get a job and start earning again.

"You could buy back Mum's share of Frederick & Green. I know Uncle Walter would love to have you," Sarah said, pulling back slightly to look her in the eye as she spoke.

Trying to ignore the hope that shone from her sister's face, Maggie shook her head. She certainly wasn't about to tell her sister that Walter had already made the offer. "I can't earn anywhere near enough there."

"And what do you need to earn so much money for?" Sarah asked, raising her eyebrows in a way that made it clear she knew exactly what the answer was.

"You know why I need to earn what I do," Maggie said, frowning; this was an old argument and not one she wanted to get into on Sarah's wedding day.

"Evie, will you do me a favour? Go and get me the flowered file box from the top of the bookcase in the lounge?" Sarah asked.

Maggie opened her mouth to protest; this was not the time for digging out God only knew what, although at least Evie was still in her dressing gown. They had all agreed that keeping her out of her beautiful bridesmaid gown until the very last minute was a must if the dress was going to make it to the church intact.

"Hello?" Grace's voice floated up the stairs.

"They're upstairs," answered Evie, who was halfway down the stairs, before Maggie or Sarah could speak.

Knowing the debate was shelved for the time being, Maggie smoothed her face and turned to smile at Grace as she entered the bedroom.

"Oh, you both look beautiful," Grace said. "I can't wait to see you in your dresses."

"You look wonderful, Grace," Sarah said, wrapping her arms around the woman who was about to become her mother-in-law, but who in all truthfulness had already been far more than that to both Maggie and Sarah for a very long time. Grace truly did look wonderful in her elegant grey dress, her bobbed hair immaculate.

"Your parents would be so proud of you both," Grace said, dabbing at the corner of her eyes.

"Here you are, Mum," Evie said, handing over a dust-covered box, and breaking the moment before all three women could fall apart.

"Thanks, pumpkin," Sarah said, before sitting on the bed and pulling off the lid. Rifling through the box, she pulled out two small plastic-covered books and handed them over to Maggie.

Maggie took them from Sarah, registering the name of the local building society on the front of them.

"Why are you showing me these?" Maggie asked.

"Just open them," Sarah said.

Slipping the first book out of its plastic sleeve, she opened it to the front page. Evie's name was printed in the patchy block text of an old printer. Flicking through the pages, she could see monthly payments had been made to the account going back for years.

"Why are you showing me Evie's savings account?" Maggie asked again.

"I have a savings account?" Evie squealed, grabbing the book from Maggie. "How much money do I have? Can I spend it?"

"Open the other one," Sarah said, nodding at the book Maggie still held in her hand.

Maggie glanced at Grace, who looked as mystified as she felt. Slipping the second book out of its sleeve, she opened the first page and saw her own name printed there. "What? How can I have a bank account I don't know about?" she asked as she turned the page and took in the date of the first payment. "Mum and Dad?" she asked.

"Yes, they set us both an account up just before, well, you know…" Sarah tripped over the words.

Flicking through the pages, Maggie realised that her parents hadn't added much to the account; there had been less than a hundred pounds in it by the time they had died. That didn't explain the payments that had started up again years later, or the size of the balance now.

"I haven't been in to get the book updated for a while, so there is a bit more in it than it shows there," Sarah said.

"I'm rich," Evie shouted, waving her own book around. "I'm going to buy a pony, and a catapult, and the biggest bag of sweets you've ever seen."

Grace laughed at Evie's enthusiasm.

"Young lady, you will be doing no such thing," Sarah said, with a smile for her daughter as she spoke. "Your Auntie Maggie has given you all that money, and you will be saving it so you can go to university."

Maggie blinked hard at the words; she hadn't given Evie anything, well, not directly. She'd been sending money to Sarah ever since she'd got her first permanent job, wanting to help her sister and niece in any way she could.

Opening the book in her hands again, Maggie flicked to the page that showed the first of the restarted payments. That first new entry must have been made just days after she'd transferred the first bit of money to Sarah's bank account. Flicking to the last page with entries on it, she took in the total and mentally added the total she'd seen in Evie's book. Sarah couldn't have used a penny of the money she'd been sending her.

"I hope you don't mind that I put some away for Evie?" Sarah asked, a tightness around her eyes and jaw.

"But … but I sent it for you."

Sarah stood up and moved over to Maggie, and kneeling in front of her she took her hands in her own. "Maggie, my wonderful little sister, I don't need your money. Paul and I have always managed just fine."

"But, you didn't go to university because of me, you couldn't get a good job, I was helping," Maggie said, her words tumbling out as she tried to explain, tried to understand.

"I don't regret any of those decisions, and I like my job, for now anyway," Sarah said with a gentle smile. "I couldn't get you to take the money back, so I just tucked it away for you, well, and for Evie too."

"But I have to pay you back," Maggie said, looking to Grace for support, for her agreement. Surely Grace would understand that she had to pay Sarah back for everything she had sacrificed? But Grace just met her look with one filled with so much sadness and understanding that Maggie had to look away. Studying her hands, wrapped in Sarah's, she swallowed hard, tears flowing down her cheeks. "I have to pay you back," she whispered.

"You don't owe me anything, Maggie. I don't want or need your money. I just need you. I need you in my life. We all do."

Maggie looked up at the matching tears that streamed down her sister's face.

"No matter where you go, no matter what happens, I will always be here for you. If you keep sending me your money, I will just keep putting it safely away for you to have back one day, but I would prefer it if that day was now."

Evie flung her arms around them both, dragging the three of them together. "Thank you for my money, Auntie Maggie, but I don't need any more either."

Maggie wrapped her arms around her sister and her niece. She didn't need the money, well, she might if she couldn't sort another job out, but in her heart she knew she'd be fine, one way or another, without it. Yet, feeling her family wrapped around her, she couldn't help but touch the surface of the book that rested in her lap. It represented something far more important than money, and while she couldn't quite put her finger on what that was, she felt a lightness she didn't ever remember experiencing.

"Come here, Grace," Sarah said, pulling the older woman into the group hug.

They stayed holding each other for a while, and Maggie let herself enjoy the sensation of being surrounded by the women she loved, before Grace pulled back.

"Well, my wonderful girls, we have a wedding to get ready for, and I think we might need to redo all of our make-up," Grace said, pulling a laugh from Maggie.

CHAPTER SEVENTEEN

Giving Sarah's hand a final squeeze, Maggie turned and stepped through the massive doorway into the church. The place was crowded with faces she knew from her childhood, and a bunch of people she didn't know.

Despite Sarah's efforts to transform the church with the gathered bunches of white flowers at the end of each pew, and the tall stand of flowers at the end of aisle, the church was still recognisably the same one that they had been to for more events for their friends and family over the years than Maggie could remember. It was still the church they had said goodbye to their parents in. No, she wasn't going to let that memory overshadow today. Today was all about the joy of her sister finally marrying the man who had worshipped her for their entire adult lives.

The memories of Paul's efforts to persuade Sarah to marry him made Maggie smile and, giving Evie a nudge to start walking up the aisle, she moved her gaze from the fittings of the church to the man standing at the end of the aisle, looking handsome, if awkward, in his morning suit. His smile as he watched his daughter make her way towards him, gently tossing white rose petals onto the floor as she went, warmed Maggie's heart.

As Maggie reached the top of the aisle she moved to the side, smiling at Evie when her niece slipped her small hand into hers. Looking up, Maggie forced herself not to look past Paul, to where his brothers stood. As he'd been unable to choose just one brother, all four of them stood at his side, a collective group of best men.

The bridal march started and, glad of the excuse to turn her gaze towards the entrance of the church, Maggie waited for her sister to enter, smiling at the collective sigh that filled the church as Sarah appeared. The dress that had looked beautiful at the fitting and again this morning, now looked extraordinary, transformed by the joy on Sarah's face as she looked at the man she was about to marry. Maggie turned to look at Paul, all signs of his earlier awkwardness gone. Instead, he looked happier than she thought she'd ever seen anyone look.

Without instruction from her brain, Maggie's eyes flicked to the side, barely registering Chris as her gaze moved on, until she met Nathan's blue eyes. The intensity as he held her gaze made her swallow and look away, unable to bear the scrutiny for another heartbeat.

Watching her sister as she took her place next to Paul, Maggie had to blink back her tears. She wanted this, one day, she wanted to stand here with someone who loved her enough to promise their whole life to her, but she knew it would never happen. She couldn't let it happen.

"I, Sarah Jane Green, do take you, Paul Albert Parker, to have and to hold from this day forward, for better, for worse, for richer, for poorer, in sickness and in health, to love and to cherish, till death us do part…"

Despite her earlier intentions, Maggie couldn't stop her eyes from drifting to Nathan. He was the man she'd imagined standing here with, and now, no matter how much she wanted it, she knew she would never be able to believe that anyone could say those words to her and mean them, especially now that the 'in sickness and in health' resonated so deeply.

Paul winked at Sarah as she finished her vows, the small smile he gave the woman he loved settling deep into Maggie. There was a man who would stand by his words. Somehow, she could believe, deep in her soul, that Paul would never leave Sarah, not by choice anyway, and despite the pang of regret that she would never have that, she was delighted that her sister could have this security.

CHAPTER EIGHTEEN

"Thank you both for making me the happiest man in the world."

Sitting across from Paul, Nathan raised his glass to join the toast. It had taken him the best part of a decade, but Paul had finally convinced Sarah that they belonged together. Watching his brother sip from his own flute as he toasted both his bride and his daughter pulled a smile from Nathan. That, just that. He finally understood what he wanted. Unfortunately, it seemed he was even slower than his brother. He turned to watch Maggie, her eyes glistening with tears as she raised her own glass and drank to her new brother-in-law's toast. A part of his life since they were old enough to toddle around with each other, Maggie was what was missing, and he'd screwed things up. Now she was with Dean, and he had to decide whether to fight or withdraw. If it had been anyone but one of his own brothers, he wouldn't have hesitated. *Damn it*, he was a fool.

Pulling at his collar, Nathan absentmindedly loosened his tie and stretched his legs under the circular table. Outwardly his attention was directed at Clive, a friend of his parents, who was chatting to him about his plans to go skiing for New Year, but inwardly every cell in his body was focused on Maggie. Her presence seemed to call to him from across the room. The fact Dean's arm was casually slung around Maggie's shoulders as the pair chatted to some of Sarah's friends wasn't helping. He wanted to stalk over there and rip his brother's arm off. It was taking all of his concentration to manage a polite nod here and there while Clive blathered on about the price of ski lifts, evidently something he expected Nathan to be equally shocked about. Thank God the man talked so much that there was no danger of Nathan being required to contribute to the conversation at any point.

The reception was in full swing, and he definitely hadn't had nearly enough to drink. His gaze was drawn back to Maggie, her head tilting back as she laughed. Her joy was like a punch to his gut. How could she be so happy when he was torn apart inside? He almost smacked himself in the face. What the hell was wrong with him that he would resent her happiness? He should be pleased she'd recovered from whatever had upset her so badly the day before. She deserved a hell of a lot better than him, that much was certain; she deserved someone who would see her worth and fight for her, not someone who'd been stupid enough to walk away.

"You could come next year." Clive's voice permeated his thoughts.

"Sorry, Clive," Nathan said, with a smile that felt as fake as his interest in the man's conversation. "It's been a long day, what did you say?"

"Next year. Come skiing with us. It's a great way to bring in the New Year."

Nathan, who up until thirty seconds ago would have said he couldn't imagine anything worse, found himself nodding. The idea of being anywhere except here next year sounded good. Thankfully, his agreement was all Clive needed before he was off again, sharing all the details of the karaoke party they went to in Austria last year.

Looking up, Nathan spotted Maggie heading across the room in his direction. He glanced around, and seeing no sign of Dean, leapt up.

"Dance with me?" he asked, before his brain could catch up with his body.

Maggie's eyes widened and she froze for what couldn't have been more than a fraction of a second, but it was long enough for him to worry she would turn him down.

"Okay," she said quietly.

The relief that filled him at her reply made Nathan realise how much he wanted to dance with her, how much he wanted the excuse to hold her in his arms again. He reached for her hand and, revelling in the soft warmth of her palm, led her to the dancefloor. As they made their way between the other couples there, he turned and pulled her into his arms, fighting a groan at the feel of her body as it brushed against his. Maggie was being careful to keep some space between them, but the occasional contact as they swayed to the romantic melody teased his senses, making him long for more. He met her gaze, and the longing that greeted him made him pull her closer. He let out a deep sigh; the feeling of her body pressed against his was perfection. It made him want to drag her off the dancefloor and into some dark corner where she would be for his eyes only, somewhere he could tell her everything she meant to him. Why was he fighting this? He wanted to be a part of her life again. He wanted to make her the centre of his life. Was she really in love with Dean? Could he walk away if she was?

"It was a lovely wedding," Maggie said, breaking the silence between them.

Damn it, she was resorting to small talk, something she had only ever done when she was really uncomfortable, or taking the mickey out of someone.

"It was. I'm really pleased for them."

"I'm glad Sarah finally said yes," she said, her smile evident, despite the fact her face was half hidden against his chest.

"Some things are worth waiting for," Nathan said. "I used to wonder if that would have been us," he added when she didn't reply, unable to stop himself.

Maggie looked up at him, eyes wide. In her silence, Nathan took the time to really look at her, to really look at this wonderful woman who had stolen his heart all those years ago. Some of her make-up had faded and dark circles were starting to show under her eyes. Her expression was frozen, almost haunted. He should have realised how exhausted she was. Instead, he'd been focused on his own thoughts and feelings. He wanted to be better than this. She made him want to be better.

Blinking, Nathan looked up, pulling Maggie's head to his chest, his eyes catching sight of Dean standing in the doorway to the bar. His brother gave him a smug grin before turning and walking out of the hall. No wonder she was exhausted. Forget the fact she'd been juggling running the accountancy firm with being in full-on wedding assistant mode since the moment she arrived, here he was trying to take her away from his own brother. They might not have seen each other for years, but the sense of loyalty and strength of character that had made her so appealing all those years ago hadn't changed. It was rooted so deeply in her that she would never forgive him for trying to make her choose, no matter what her decision was. He sucked in a deep breath and steeled himself.

"I'm sorry, I should have said that to you before. I should have told you how sorry I am for what happened between us. I'm glad that Dean makes you happy, though," Nathan said, the words cracking in his throat as he forced them out.

Maggie's head snapped up and she stared at him, slack-jawed, for a few seconds. No longer moving in time to the music, she stood, frozen in place. As his words sank in her expression changed, a frown forming before she pulled away and abruptly stepped back. Almost imperceptibly she shook her head, before turning and dashing away, moving so fast that he could almost convince himself that those hadn't been tears in her eyes.

Nathan balled his hands up at his sides. Tension filled him as he tried to believe he had done the right thing. *Damn it*, for all he knew Maggie was just annoyed he thought his opinion mattered. Well, no matter what, she was unhappy now and he wasn't about to leave her on her own.

He stalked out of the hall and into the bar, where he found Dean sitting with their other brothers and respective partners.

"You might want to catch up with Maggie," he growled at Dean.

"Why?" Dean asked, his forehead wrinkling into a frown.

"I think she's upset."

"What did you do to her?" Dean asked coldly.

"That doesn't matter," Nathan all but shouted. The fact that Dean was right on the money simply ratcheted his frustration up further.

Dean laughed at his obvious temper, the sound harsh and unamused, but he didn't move.

"Maggie is upset — are you seriously going to leave her on her own?"

"Do you really think you get to tell me how to treat Maggie?" Dean asked, standing up.

"I'll go see if she's okay," Paula said, lifting herself out of the low couch. "I could do with another wee anyway. Damn baby is sitting on my bladder."

Nathan murmured his thanks, but couldn't bring himself to look away from Dean. His brother was keeping Maggie from him, and the man wasn't even considerate enough to go and check up on her.

"She deserves better," Nathan said flatly.

"What, like you?" Dean asked, shifting into Nathan's space. "Leaving her alone and upset is your trademark move, so don't start with me."

"You bastard," Nathan said, and without any instruction from his brain he raised his fist and swung. The crack as it connected with his brother's cheek brought a surge of satisfaction that built as he watched Dean stagger backwards, attempting to maintain his balance.

"What the hell?" Dean exclaimed, stalking forward to repay the favour.

Bring it on, Nathan thought. It was going to take a lot more than one punch for him to feel any better. Ten might do it.

"Boys."

Oh God, Nathan thought at the flat sound of disappointment in his mum's voice. Was there anything worse than being caught fighting by your mum? It didn't matter that he was an adult. It didn't matter that he and his brothers had spent years fighting each other, despite the fact they loved each other. He hated letting his mum down. With a groan he forced his arms down to his sides and, head dipped, turned to face her.

"What is going on? Why are you two fighting?"

"Maggie," Joe piped up, his amusement obvious despite his efforts to hide it.

Grace looked from Joe back to Dean and Nathan, her expression softening when she looked at Nathan. Hell, he must look bad if she was letting him off after punching Dean.

She turned her face to Dean. "Tell him," she said.

Tell him what? What was going on? Not only had she not reamed them out for fighting, but she had pulled out that voice. The one all mums seem to have that ensures total obedience. Nathan's head swung between his mum and brother.

Dean nodded at their mum before turning to Nathan. "She's not my girlfriend," he said with a sigh.

Nathan just stared at him, uncomprehending. What was he on about? His confusion must have shown in his expression as Dean spoke again.

"Maggie is not my girlfriend, we're not together," he said with a shrug.

Nathan felt something shift inside him. A crushing weight that he hadn't realised existed, lifted, and he felt as though he could breathe properly. "But, you said…" he mumbled, not sure how to articulate his jumbled thoughts.

"No," Dean said. "Neither of us said it. You assumed, and I let you."

Nathan turned to his mum, and she gave him a small smile. "But," Nathan started and then stopped abruptly. Thinking back, he realised no one had said it. There had been hints, and he knew his mum had thought it too. But it was true, no one had said it. "Why did you let me think it? Why did you let us all think it?"

Dean looked at him, his fingertips gingerly touching his cheek where a red mark was blooming. "You hurt her. She was worried about seeing you again, so I just let you assume."

Nathan felt the truth of his brother's words sink deep inside him. It might have been years ago, but he had hurt Maggie. He'd hurt her and then run away, too scared to face the consequence of his actions, too afraid to see what he had done to her, and to himself. He had thought, hoped, that after all this time, he could try again, and the whole time, she had been simply trying to hold herself together.

Remembering what he had said to her on the dancefloor, Nathan groaned. What the hell was wrong with him? He'd done it again. He'd pushed her away just as she was coming to him.

He sank into an armchair, letting his head flop backward as he tried to absorb everything. Maggie wasn't with Dean. She had danced with him and he had pushed her towards Dean — was that was why she had been upset? She thought he didn't want her. Nathan snapped his head back up and stared at his mum.

"Maggie isn't with Dean," he said to her, feeling the grin that spread across his mouth.

"No, she's not," Grace replied with a gentle smile.

"I have to go," he said, getting up and heading for the exit.

"She's in the hall," Grace said, pointing back to the doors where the disco music was still pounding.

"I know, but I need to figure out how to fix this. I have to get this right," Nathan said, deep in thought. Leaning down, he gently kissed his mum's cheek. "I'll see you tomorrow."

CHAPTER NINETEEN

At the sound of the main door opening, Maggie glanced up from the computer, blinking as her eyes adjusted and trying not to groan at the interruption. She'd been staring at the same spreadsheet for at least an hour, and it had finally felt like she was making progress.

"Nathan Parker, what are you doing here?" Susie said, her voice far warmer than Maggie had heard it since Walter had been away.

"Good to see you, Susie. I was just hoping for a quick word with Maggie."

As he spoke, Nathan crossed the office and stood in the doorway, giving Maggie a chance to take in his dust-covered jeans and arms, but almost spotless T-shirt. He'd clearly pulled it on when he'd stopped whatever he'd been working on, and the thought of him working with a bare chest had her shifting in her chair.

When he continued to just stand there, one hand behind his back, Maggie cleared her throat. She didn't want to engage with him, but she didn't think she could take the silence. Silence was usually one of her special skills; she was comfortable enough with it that she could always get the other party to crack first, something that was a big part of why she was so successful at work. Now, though? Now all she could think about was the text Dean had sent her on his way home. The fact that Nathan knew she was pathetic enough to let him believe she was dating his brother bounced around her head.

"Did you want something?" Maggie finally asked.

"You look like you belong there," Nathan said, a smile curling the corner of his mouth, tightening his skin and highlighting the scar on his chin that she'd always loved.

Glancing down at the desk, Maggie smiled. "I didn't think I'd be able to sit here," she admitted. She'd been surprised by the sense of peace she'd found sitting at her mother's desk when she'd worked up the courage to do it.

"You can do anything you set your mind to, you always could," Nathan said, stepping into the office, the smile on his face softening and making Maggie swallow hard.

It felt like a long time since she'd been the girl he remembered.

Pulling his hand out from behind his back he held his palm out, and pink icing gleamed at her from the top of a bright red cupcake.

"Red velvet? You bought me a red velvet cupcake? From Tess's Bakery?" Maggie asked, the treat distracting her from the dangerous direction his comment had taken her thoughts.

"Yes, I hope they're still your favourite?"

"Gimme," Maggie said, standing and leaning over the desk to reach it.

Nathan let her take it with a warm laugh.

She didn't bother trying to speak; she just shoved the sugary goodness into her mouth, leaning back and closing her eyes with pleasure.

"Okay, definitely still a favourite."

"You have no idea how much I needed this," Maggie said around a mouthful of sponge, as she brushed the crumbs from her blazer. It had felt strange at first to be at work without a full suit on. She hadn't been able to go as far as wearing her jeans into the office, but the blazer and blouse felt like a compromise.

"I didn't actually pop in just to ply you with cake," Nathan said.

"I should have known," she said, her heart stopping as she waited for him to bring up her attempt to seem like she wasn't a total loser.

"Actually, I thought I'd see if you wanted me to pick Evie up from school?"

Maggie looked at him for a beat before realising he was being genuine, that he wasn't about to call her out, not right now anyway. "That would be great, if you don't mind. I have so much to get through. I'd always imagined working in a little rural office would be calm and quiet, but I don't think Uncle Walter can ever come up for air."

"He definitely works hard," Nathan said, stepping away from her with a smile. "I'll feed Evie so you don't have to rush home."

Maggie's heart lurched; home, that was something she'd always dreamed they'd have together. This kind of ordinary conversation would be normal for them, the sort of conversation any husband and wife would have about their own child. Now it was the sort of conversation she wasn't sure she'd ever be able to have. She gave him a smile of thanks before shoving the last of the sumptuous cake into her mouth, saving herself from having to find the words to reply.

"You know he has his own work to be doing," Susie said, once Nathan had left the office.

Maggie looked up at Susie; the girl might be petite, but she still managed to loom. She wrinkled her brow, wondering where Susie was going with her statement.

"Nathan," Susie said, gesturing to the now empty doorway. "He has his own work to finish, and you have him running around doing what you told Sarah you'd do."

Maggie's jaw tightened. Susie had been snarky with her from the minute she'd stepped back into the office. "What is your point?"

"You're taking advantage of him."

"He offered to pick his niece up from school; how is that taking advantage?"

Susie didn't answer, just looked at her, eyebrows raised, as though expecting her to make some sort of deductive leap. Maggie waited for a moment, wondering if Susie was going to enlighten her any further.

"You know what, this really isn't any of your business," Maggie said softly, realising she didn't want to get into it.

She might wish that things were easy with Susie again, but it was becoming clear the woman had only ever been friendly to her because Dean had insisted on hanging out with Nathan, and Maggie was a part of the package.

"Have you finished inputting the Fetheringstone account details?"

"Not yet," Susie said, wandering back into the main office area with a roll of her eyes.

Well, Maggie wasn't going to be making friends there anytime soon, but if she was honest, she didn't have the energy to care. She had three days to get through five days' work, if she was going to be able to have her surgery, and recover, without letting Uncle Walter down.

As Maggie pushed open the door to the cottage, the warmth inside wrapped around her. Her stomach rumbled as she registered the scent of spiced meat. It had been hours since she'd eaten, and she really should have made it home earlier than eight-thirty, but she'd been determined to wrap up the accounts she'd been working on before calling it a night.

Slipping her coat off and placing it on the bannister, she headed towards the source of the enticing smell, preparing to grovel to Nathan for abusing his help by being so late.

As she reached the kitchen doorway, she stopped dead at the sight of Nathan, his back to her as he stirred a pot on the hob. Barefoot, his jeans still covered in dust, his thin T-shirt was doing nothing to hide the muscles flexing in his back and shoulders as he moved.

"Sorry I'm so late," Maggie said, her voice husky.

Turning to face her, Nathan tossed a tea towel to rest on his shoulder and smiled warmly. "It's no problem. Evie has just gone to bed." His eyes travelled up her body with a slight frown. "If you want to say goodnight to her, you can get out of your work clothes while I serve up?"

Maggie fought the urge to fidget under his clearly unimpressed scrutiny. The blazer and trousers were some of her favourite clothes. She nodded and headed upstairs. Surely when most men asked you to get out of your work clothes, it was for more than the fact they didn't like the outfit? Standing at the top of the stairs, she leant against the wall. She needed to get a grip. Nathan clearly wasn't any more interested in her now than he had been when she'd thrown herself at him all those years ago. Unfortunately, she didn't even have the benefit of hiding behind the idea he believed she was with Dean anymore. He knew she wasn't, and he still wasn't interested.

Well, at least he was feeding her, she thought. Whatever he was cooking smelled far better than the mushroom risotto ready meal she'd been planning to microwave.

After peeking in to say goodnight to a smiling but sleepy Evie, Maggie slipped on her favourite pair of velour lounge pants and a T-shirt that she found buried at the bottom of her drawers. She probably hadn't worn it since she'd officially moved out of the cottage at the end of university. She smiled at the thought of her sister keeping all her belongings in what was now essentially the spare room for her. The room had been redecorated, and had been used by Sarah and Paul's friends far more than Maggie had used it in the last few years, but they still called it Maggie's room.

"I always loved that T-shirt," Nathan said, taking her in with a smile, his earlier disapproval gone. "Okay, I've made a lamb tagine, although technically, it's not really a tagine as I made it on the hob."

"You can call it whatever you like, it smells fantastic." As they sat together at the small kitchen table, Maggie tucked in, letting out a groan as the explosion of flavours hit her tongue. "Wow. That is incredible. How did you learn to cook like this? Last time I checked, beans on toast was about your speed."

"I'm still fairly limited," Nathan replied, and she spared him a disbelieving glance before turning her attention back to the food. "I picked up a few recipes when I was travelling; learning to cook with the locals was a great experience."

"You can cook for me anytime," she said.

"In which case, I hope you really like it because I only have about five other recipes to my name, so you'd get it a lot."

Maggie smiled at him, the back and forth feeling a lot like the way their relationship used to work. She'd had enough of overthinking things. Tonight she just wanted to enjoy the evening.

Sipping her glass of wine, Maggie let out a sigh as she curled her legs up on the couch. Her phone buzzed and she picked it up, the text from Dean dropping her spirits, something his messages never did, and a reaction she knew was all about the reminder it contained, and nothing to do with the person sending it.

So, have you managed to avoid Nathan?

After the wedding, Dean had headed back to London first thing on the Sunday morning, which, combined with his refusal to use his phone to actually speak to other people, meant she hadn't been able to interrogate him about exactly what had been said between him and his brother on the night of the wedding. Somehow, over the last couple of hours, Nathan had relaxed her enough that she'd completely forgotten to be on edge about her unintentional deception.

"Is everything okay?" Nathan asked, sitting next to her, a glass in his own hand.

"Just a text from Dean," Maggie said, wishing she could bite her tongue the second the words slipped out. Why did she have to remind him of the elephant in the room?

Not quite, he cooked for me this evening... she texted back, adding a stunned face emoji.

"Is he okay?" Nathan asked.

"I assume so. He was just checking on me," she said, watching the ellipsis at the bottom of her screen that told her Dean was replying so she could avoid looking at Nathan.

"I'm glad you have each other for support in London," he said.

Maggie's head swung up at the sincerity in his tone. "Really?" she asked, unable to keep the scepticism from her voice.

Nathan smiled at her, that lopsided smile that had always felt like it was just for her. "Really. I admit, I might have jumped to some conclusions that made it hard to see the pair of you so close, but I am glad he's been there for you."

The, *when I wasn't*, remained silent, but it was as though Nathan was transmitting the thought directly into her brain.

"Why would Dean and I being close matter?" Maggie asked, knowing she should just shut up. There were some questions that just shouldn't be asked, but she couldn't help herself. Nathan had made it clear that he didn't want her, so why would he care if he thought she was with his brother?

"It shouldn't," he said, and her heart sank. "I'd better go," he added, as he leant over and placed a kiss on the top of her head before walking out of the room.

Maggie fought the urge to ask him to stay. What would be the point? Whether it was now or later didn't make any difference — he was going to leave.

CHAPTER TWENTY

Pulling up outside the barn the following evening, Nathan switched off his truck engine. He started to unbuckle his seatbelt, and then stopped, suddenly not quite sure this was a good idea. Forcing himself to look across at a silent Maggie, he tried not to notice her almost translucent complexion as she stared blankly at the outline of the barn, which was barely visible in the pale moonlight. He'd been so excited to bring her here and share his plans, but now that they were here, he wondered whether he was about to undo all the progress he'd made over the last couple of days.

"I need to get some outside lighting rigged up," he said, needing to break the silence. It wasn't like he could turn around and drive Maggie straight home, so he needed to get over whatever was going on in his brain.

"It hasn't changed at all," Maggie said, the words so quiet he almost missed them.

"I hope you think differently when you see the inside," Nathan said. "I've replaced a lot of the stones and mortaring out here, but you can't see that in the dark. To be fair it's not that obvious in the day either, which is frustrating given how long it took and how much it cost."

She gave him a weak smile and climbed out of the truck.

Dashing around to her side of the truck so he could use his torch to light her way to the door, Nathan clenched his fist. Why had he thought this was a good idea? They'd finally been getting along. He'd picked Evie up from school and made dinner for Maggie for the last two days, and their friendship seemed to be flourishing again. He was going to run out of recipes before long, but Maggie didn't seem to care about that. The first night, he'd left rather than admit to her he'd been jealous of his brother, but last night he'd stayed longer, the pair of them relaxing on the couch, half watching the TV as they chatted. He desperately wanted to share this part of his life with her, so it had been easy for the invitation to come and visit the barn to slip from his lips. Now, taking in her pale, tight expression, and the way she wrapped her arms tightly around her body, he was regretting it. It wasn't like they could forever ignore the fact he'd bought the barn without her, but he should have let their burgeoning friendship solidify before testing it like this.

A couple of steps from the door, Maggie stumbled. Nathan's arm shot out, curling around her elbow to steady her. For a moment he thought she was going to let him hold her, but as soon as she was fully upright she pulled back, her elbow slipping from his grip with an urgency that left a heaviness in his chest.

"Let's see what you've done, then," she said, her obvious effort to inject some enthusiasm into her words falling flat.

Opening the door, Nathan flicked on the lights. "The electricity isn't set up in every room, but it works in this half of the barn," he said, leading Maggie through.

He watched her with a smile as she ran her hands down the smooth, bare plaster covering the walls.

"This will be the kitchen," he said, as they entered the open space that currently held a decorator's table, on which his small selection of crockery and cutlery was stacked next to a well-used microwave and kettle.

"Well, I can see why you like cooking at the cottage so much," Maggie said.

"Yes, Sarah's kitchen equipment is definitely the reason," Nathan replied with a half-smile.

Leading her on before she could comment, he gestured awkwardly to his bedroom. The mattress on the bare floor, duvet thrown back from when he'd risen that morning, looked bleak as he took it in with Maggie at his side. Her presence made him realise that, even when he finally managed to paint the walls, and fill the rooms with proper furniture, it would feel just as empty as it was now.

"Just as tidy as ever, then," she said with a giggle.

"We can't all be neat freaks," Nathan said, gesturing to her outfit that included yet another perfectly pressed pair of tailored trousers and immaculate heels.

"No one would ever accuse you of that," Maggie said. "Anyway, there's nothing wrong with wanting to be smart."

"Maggie, you take it way beyond looking smart. It's like you're wearing armour."

His disappointment that she'd reverted from the casual clothes of the last couple of evenings meant his words came out without thought, but the way Maggie flinched made him wonder just how close to the truth he had come. What was she protecting herself from?

"Come and see the rest," he said, grabbing her hand and leading her away, before she could sink further into the gloom that was threatening to reappear.

Entering his work area, Nathan reluctantly let go of her hand so he could kneel. Using the light of his torch, he reconnected the plug on the floor. As he slipped it into place, the whole room was lit by the industrial lighting rigs he had placed around the space. It wasn't exactly a cosy atmosphere, but it gave him enough light to work at any time of day or night.

"Wow," Maggie said. "This is where we used to roll around on our skateboards, isn't it?" she asked, moving across the cluttered space, and touching the new window that he'd added to the previously open wall. They had spent more days than he could remember climbing in and out of the massive space that was now glassed in.

"Yes, it's my workshop now."

Maggie moved around the room, taking in the various pieces that he had spread throughout the space. Reaching the corner where he stacked the wood blanks, she reached out, touching them tentatively. "You turn this, into that?" she asked, gesturing from the raw material to one of the finished chairs without turning to face him.

"I do," Nathan said. "I know it's not very glamorous, but I enjoy it."

He felt that odd sensation of embarrassment that he wasn't used to experiencing with Maggie. Some part of him wanted to impress her, but he wasn't sure that this new, polished Maggie would be impressed by anything except for the sort of city traders she must be used to these days.

Her head bobbed before she moved, her fingers trailing delicately along the frame of one of the set of chairs he had just finished. He needed to get on with the drawings and sample pieces he'd need for his meeting with Andersson Hotels, but he'd promised the client who'd ordered the chairs that they'd have them in time for Christmas lunch, and he wasn't about to start letting people down on the off chance of a big deal, no matter how life-changing.

Maggie lifted her phone from her pocket, smiling at whatever message she'd received before tapping out a quick reply and slipping it back out of sight. Nathan kept his expression smooth, despite the fact that he'd like to throw the damn thing across the room. He knew she must have other friends, but he suspected it was Dean again. The fact his brother messaged her so often was driving him slowly crazy. He was the Parker she was supposed to be closest to, not his brother. Knowing that they weren't in a romantic relationship didn't seem to be helping his jealousy. If anything, the tight knot that formed in his chest at every reminder of the distance between them was getting worse.

Maggie moved over to what Nathan laughingly called his office area and began to study the drawings spread out on his massive drafting table. It was one of the only proper pieces of furniture he owned. He'd picked it up dirt cheap at an auction, and at the time he'd felt guilty, spending money he didn't really have to waste. Now, he was really glad he'd bought it. Completing as many designs as he needed to ahead of his meeting with Andersson Hotels would be damned hard without it.

"You drew these?" Maggie asked.

"Yes, I have the chance of a deal with a hotel, so I'm working on some designs for them." Nathan walked across the space, picking his way between the tools and part completed items, until he stood next to her. He hadn't told anyone about the call, but somehow he couldn't imagine not telling Maggie. It might have taken him a few days, but now he'd told her, he realised that part of why he'd wanted to bring her here tonight was so he could share his news.

"You're so talented," she said, her hand slipping into his.

The warmth of her fingers flowed through him and he closed his eyes. Her words heated him as much as the contact. He'd wanted to impress her, and there was no questioning her sincerity. When he opened his eyes, she was still completely focused on the images in front of them.

"Why don't I go get us a drink while you look through the drawings?" he asked. "I'd love to hear if you have any ideas to make them better."

Maggie looked up at him, her eyes shimmering as though she understood that he'd said far more than the words he'd spoken. Nathan swallowed and resisted the urge to reach out and touch her face.

"You want my opinion?"

"Always," he said, his voice husky.

"But I don't know anything about furniture."

Nathan shook his head. "I still want to hear your thoughts. I always want to hear your thoughts."

The back of his throat felt scratchy. He gently released her hand and stepped back. He wanted nothing more than to pull her into his arms and kiss her. He wanted to be able to share everything with her. Giving her a smile, he walked away before he forgot himself and pushed too hard.

CHAPTER TWENTY-ONE

Studying the array of incredible drawings, Maggie couldn't help but smile. She'd always known Nathan would be amazing at whatever he ended up doing with his life, but the sheer talent in his drawings and his finished work, she thought, turning to glance at the coffee table next to her, was astounding. It was of moderate size with a rough-hewn finish to its slab surface, but it was the legs that really drew her attention. They had been created to make it look as though the table had simply walked out of the forest of its own accord. It was magical, and unlike anything she had ever seen before.

"Here," Nathan said, handing her a glass of red wine. "It's only cheap, but it tastes pretty good."

Maggie took the glass from him, knowing she couldn't drink much, but taking a small sip as she turned her attention back to the drawings.

"So what do you think?" he asked.

At the uncertainty in his voice, Maggie turned to face him, surprised. Was he nervous about what she'd say? "You are so talented," she said. "I've never seen furniture look like this. That hotel would be lucky to have your work."

As though amused by something, he gave her that half smile of his and her eyes wandered to his scar. She wanted to reach out and touch it. Instead, she turned back to the table of drawings, her finger tracing the lines on the huge sheets of paper, satisfying herself with touching his creations instead.

"Here, let's relax while you look at them," Nathan said, scooping the papers up with one hand as he juggled his own glass and the rest of the wine bottle with the other. Following his long strides, she joined him at the large couch he had positioned in one corner.

Brushing some of the wood dust from the fabric, Maggie sank into the couch. Nathan flicked off some of the lights, making it so the room was cast in a cosy glow, rather than the bright illumination of before, and then, instead of sitting at the other end of the long couch, he sat next to her. The heat from his body radiated into her almost immediately and she shivered. She hadn't realised how cold the large space he was using as his work room was until that warmth began to trickle into her.

Pulling a blanket from behind the couch, Nathan draped it over her. "Sorry, no heating in this area yet," he said with a shrug.

"Why do you have a couch in here? Is it your lounge as well?" Maggie asked, realising she hadn't seen a room that looked like it would become a lounge as he'd shown her around.

"I guess I kind of use it as one at the moment. It's nice to have somewhere comfy to sit when I'm stuck on something."

Maggie smiled at that, picturing a frustrated Nathan flopping on the couch when his work wasn't going as smoothly as he'd like.

She picked up her wine and slipped her shoes off, curling her legs up under the blanket. The action shifted her closer to Nathan. He moved, sliding his arm around her shoulder so she was nestled against his side. She knew she should pull away, but she didn't want to lose the heat of his body against hers. At least that was how she tried to justify herself.

They sat in companionable silence as she leafed through Nathan's drawings. Maggie couldn't help but reflect on how different the inside of the barn was from the last time she'd been in it. The single space had been split into multiple rooms, yet Nathan had managed to make it so each wall felt as though it should have always been there. She could just picture the place finished, a family home. Her heart pinched at the realisation that she wasn't the person Nathan would enjoy that with.

"So, you and Dean hang out a lot?" Nathan asked into the silence.

Maggie's hand tightened around her glass. Was he finally going to call her out on her behaviour? She surely deserved it; after all, letting him think she was dating his brother wasn't the most mature thing to have done. "Yes," she said slowly. "He's been a good friend to me. I was in a relationship with someone else. Dean has been helping me through the break-up."

"I'm glad," Nathan said and she shifted, turning so she could look at him with a frown. Taking in her expression, he smiled gently at her. "I'm not glad you have been hurt, but I'm glad my annoying brother was there to help you. Mostly I'm glad that you and Dean aren't together. I don't think I could have taken it."

"Why?" Maggie asked, her frown deepening.

What did it matter to Nathan if she had been dating Dean? She'd been happy to let him think it, but only to protect her own self-respect. The thought of him knowing how crap her life had become had been too much to cope with. Looking back, it had been foolish, but she'd never imagined that he would care.

"You know why," Nathan said, shifting so he could smooth her hair back from her forehead.

Maggie shook her head without really knowing why. The desire in his eyes took away any doubt about his reasons, but part of her wanted to hear it. Inside a small voice was shouting at her to stop, to pull back. It wasn't like anything they could have would last. Even if she was naïve enough to believe it could last, she certainly couldn't offer him any kind of future when she didn't know if she even had a future. The thought reminded her of what she was facing in the morning, so she shook it off.

"Maggie, I love you. I have always loved you."

At his words, her eyes filled. She'd longed to hear those words from him since she'd been a teenager. She'd wanted to hear them, wanted him to say them back to her when she'd declared her love for him the only time they had made love, and now he was finally saying them, they seemed to tear something vital from deep within her heart.

"Please don't cry, Maggie. I've made you cry more times than I should be forgiven for, but I'm begging you to forgive me. I walked away from you once, and I've spent years running from that mistake. I'm sorrier than I can ever say."

"You don't even know me anymore," Maggie said, the tears spilling over her lashes and down her cheeks.

Nathan cupped her cheek with his hand, and she didn't resist as his other arm pulled her closer, holding her gaze. "I know you, Maggie Green. I know every part of you. I know your soul and I know we should be together. We should make a life together, have a family together. We should fill this barn with our love and laughter, with the laughter of our children."

He stared at her intently as he spoke, as though willing her to believe him. Maggie swallowed, trying to find a response when she didn't know how to put the truth into words. It was everything she'd ever dreamed of, and it was a future she couldn't deliver.

"If I wasn't enough for you then, I'm certainly not now," she whispered.

She couldn't tell him. Wouldn't tell him. Despite the fact that every cell in her body was screaming at her to be honest, that he would understand and be there for her. But that was what she was afraid of. He'd stand by her side as she faced her own mortality. He'd stand by her side if she survived and found she couldn't give him the family he wanted. He'd stand by her side, even though she would be destroying the future he wanted. Then one day, when she finally let herself believe it could last, he would leave. Everyone left in the end.

Nathan leant closer, and despite the voice inside shouting at her to move, Maggie found she couldn't. As his head dipped, she remained in place, and when his lips met hers, the voice in her head shut down completely. They didn't have a future together, she might not have a future at all, but there was this moment, and she was sick of fighting what she wanted.

When Nathan took the glass from her hand, Maggie didn't resist. Instead, she curled her now empty hand around his neck and drew him closer. The smooth flavour of the wine remained on his lips, but as their kiss deepened, her senses were flooded with the flavour of the man she had loved since she had been a child. As she opened her lips with a sigh, he swept his tongue into her mouth and pulled her onto his lap.

"I'm so sorry I hurt you," Nathan whispered as his lips teased along the column of her neck.

Maggie had wanted to hear those words for so long, and she knew he regretted hurting her, that was just the kind of man he was, but she couldn't trust that they changed anything.

She moved, attempting to haul herself from Nathan's lap, but he tightened his hold on her waist and pulled her back closer. Resting his forehead on hers, he screwed his eyes closed.

"I was such a fool," he said. "I've loved you all my life, Maggie Green, and when you came to me that night, I felt complete, as though everything was finally how it should be."

His words were ragged, as though he was fighting to hold himself together, but as she listened to him, the cold that she had forgotten while wrapped in his arms crept back.

Maggie pulled harder this time, slipping off his lap, and standing up as she attempted to slide her feet back into her shoes before she fell apart completely.

"Please, don't go," Nathan said as he bolted up from the couch, the plea in his voice giving her pause before she continued moving.

"If you'd loved me," Maggie whispered, "you couldn't have left me." She knew the truth of that, because there was nothing other than his rejection of her that could have made her leave him that day.

"I was scared," he said, his words almost lost to the pounding of her heart.

She froze. *Scared? Scared of what?* She looked up at him, his expression lost, his fists tight, as though trying to stop himself from reaching out to grab her.

"I didn't want you to settle for me, like Sarah had done with Paul."

"Sarah loves Paul," Maggie said with a frown.

"Well, we know that now, but back then she had no choice but to stick around when he got her pregnant."

Maggie studied him. "Why did you think I would be settling for you? I gave myself to you. I told you I loved you."

"Mum was worried you would give up your dreams for me," Nathan said, holding her gaze.

"Your mum? She knows what happened?" Maggie asked, her heart sinking at the thought of Grace knowing what a fool she had made of herself.

"No, God no. Maggie, I have never told anyone, I promise you that," he said, reaching for her hand.

Maggie studied where their hands joined, comfort easing through her at the contact, even while she fought to understand what he was telling her.

"She knew how excited I was that you were coming back for the holidays. It had only been five weeks, but I'd missed you so much. I think she knew how I felt about you long before I did," Nathan smiled at her softly. "The last day of your holidays, she warned me to be careful."

"She didn't want you to be with me?" Maggie asked, her heart pinching at the realisation that, despite how much Grace seemed to care about her, she wasn't good enough for Grace's son.

"No, she didn't; she was the one who said I shouldn't trap you like Paul had trapped Sarah."

Maggie didn't know what to say to that. Paul hadn't trapped Sarah, he'd been as caught out by the way things had happened as her sister had. Besides, it had all worked out in the end. Even through all the years Sarah had refused Paul's proposals, Maggie had known her sister had loved him. It had never been about that.

"So you just took the opportunity to leave me?" Maggie asked, not really needing an answer.

"Maggie," Nathan said, his voice cracking on her name as he stepped closer to her.

She looked up, wanting to stop him from speaking. Whatever he said, it was only going to sound like an excuse, and she didn't want to listen to excuses. As she met his deep blue eyes, the pain that shone from them caught her breath in her chest. Reaching up, she touched his face with her palm, the rough texture of his stubble teasing her senses.

Maggie didn't have the words to take his pain away, she didn't even know how to take her own away, but the realisation that it wasn't just she who had suffered tugged deep inside. Closing the distance between them, she slowly lifted her face until their lips met. The contact was so light it almost didn't exist. For a moment neither of them moved, then suddenly, as if their bodies were in complete synchronicity, the pressure changed. Hands were everywhere. Maggie hungrily pulled at Nathan's clothing, wanting to touch every part of him.

CHAPTER TWENTY-TWO

Easing a tiny gap between their bodies, Nathan flicked the buttons on Maggie's blouse open. Once he could pull the two sides of the fabric apart, he pulled back, desperate to see all of her. A pink satin bra peeked out at him and he sucked in a breath at the sight of her smooth breasts, her chest rising and falling with her rapid breaths as he slipped her blouse down her arms. Running one hand down her neck and along the line of her bra, he revelled in the warmth of her flesh. Leaning forward, he gently followed the path of his hand with a trail of kisses. Unclipping her bra, he slipped it from her shoulders, letting it fall to the ground so he could enjoy every inch of her. Easing her backwards until her knees hit the couch, he lowered her onto it, the sight of her laid out before him so precious he didn't dare close his eyes in case she was gone when he opened them again.

He wanted to spend the whole night worshipping Maggie the way she deserved. He wanted to spend his whole life doing it. The thought hit him so hard that he froze. The desire to push for that kind of commitment from her was almost overwhelming, but this wasn't the right way to do it. If he was stupid enough to propose in the midst of sex, she'd think it was the wrong part of his body doing all the thinking, but he knew with absolute certainty that it was what he wanted, what he needed. For now, he'd be content with this moment.

Easing further down her body, Nathan sprinkled feather-light kisses across her belly, enjoying the softness of her feminine curves. The only other time he'd been lucky enough to touch her like this, she had been skinny in the way only teenagers were; they both had been. Now she was all woman, and the desire he'd felt for her since hitting puberty rocketed. She pulled at his shoulders.

"Nathan." His name was like a promise, a plea on her lips, sending his blood roaring through his veins so loudly that he had to keep reminding himself to take his time, to savour being with her.

Resisting her efforts to speed things up, his hands slowly drifted to her trousers and he lowered the zip holding them in place. Maggie eased her hips off the couch, allowing him to slide her trousers and underwear down her legs and off. Sitting back on his haunches, Nathan took her in. She'd filled out, and her once unblemished skin had the inevitable marks and scars that mapped out the years since he'd last been lucky enough to see her like this, yet she was still his Maggie, and she was still perfect. Meeting her eyes, he saw the expression was more uncertain than the determined, seductive one she'd had the last time. Grown up Maggie felt more real.

Nathan swallowed back the words that once again tried to push their way out. Instead, he leant forward and kissed her ankle, he made his way up her leg, the slight stubble on her calves making him smile. Unlike the time she'd come to him before, she hadn't been expecting to take her clothes off tonight. The fact she was letting him see the cracks in her perfect image undid any intention he had of taking things slow and, pushing his way back up to her face, his lips met hers in a clash of need and hunger.

Feeling Nathan's arms relax around her, Maggie tried to keep her own body lax, but as she had drifted back from the ecstasy Nathan had delivered, his words had begun to echo in her head.

"I won't leave you, not again. Not ever."

The words had been whispered into her ear as he'd pulled her back to his chest, curling his arm around her waist and slowly drifting off to sleep. She supposed she should be jumping with joy that he finally wanted to be with her, forever if his statement was to be believed. And therein lay her problem: she didn't believe him. She didn't think he was deliberately lying about his intentions, but she knew better than to risk her heart on a whispered promise that came moments after having sex. He'd whispered all sorts of promises to her that first time, and it had taken the grand total of twelve hours for him to step back so firmly from them that she'd been left reeling for years. Under the blanket he had wrapped around them, she waited for him to fall asleep and silently hoped he still slept well enough that nothing would disturb him.

Looking around, Maggie accepted that Nathan wasn't the same person he'd been when they had both been teenagers. For one, he was making an enormous effort to put down roots, but she had changed as well. She'd worked out that she couldn't trust anyone with her heart.

Placing her hand over his, she swallowed hard. She wished she could find a way to relax and enjoy the moment. It didn't matter what either of them said. It didn't even matter if there was a way that they could make it work, a way that they could last. The reality was that she had to face tomorrow, and she was going to need all her energy to get through it.

She didn't want to have to explain to Nathan that she didn't trust him, that she didn't trust anyone. It wasn't weakness to want to avoid that conversation. It was self-preservation, because with the effort it was going to take to get through the next few days, she wasn't sure she could be strong enough to keep him at a distance. Not anymore.

Finally, unable to lie there with her own thoughts any longer, Maggie risked a quick glance over her shoulder. Cast in shadow, Nathan's face looked like it had been sculpted, the beginnings of a five o'clock shadow simply adding to his masculinity. Resisting the urge to just enjoy being where she had been dreaming of being for a long time, she shifted. Pausing after each small movement, she kept checking she hadn't disturbed him. Free of Nathan's embrace, Maggie gathered up her clothing. Skin prickling against the sudden cold, she tiptoed out of the workspace and into the hallway. Once she'd dressed, she pulled the door open, the icy cold hitting her instantly. It was only a fifteen-minute walk if she cut across the fields, but she was going to freeze in about five. Glancing around, she resisted the urge to take the keys to Nathan's truck. Giving him an excuse to come and find her too soon was a very bad idea. Spotting a pile of clothing on top of a ratty cardboard box, she rummaged until she found an old padded coat. Slipping it on, she pushed the sleeves up past her wrists so she could do up the buttons, and opened the door again. She looked ridiculous, but she was free.

CHAPTER TWENTY-THREE

Nathan winced at the crick in his neck, but even that didn't affect the smile on his face. Shifting his arm, he wiggled his fingers, finding the edge of the couch but no Maggie. Heart sinking, his eyes flew open. The dark of night was still firmly in place, but there was no sign of the woman herself. The clothes that he had stripped off her were no longer pooled on the floor. Trying to tell himself she must have gone to the bathroom, or to get a drink, he registered the cold that surrounded him. She'd been gone long enough that, even with the blanket in place, any warmth from her presence had seeped away.

Unable to accept that she'd just left, Nathan stood and pulled his jeans on, attempting to ignore his rising nausea. A quick search of the half-finished barn confirmed what he had been trying to deny. Maggie really had gone. Shit, how the hell had he screwed this up? He wanted to hunt her down and shake her until she came back. How could she just walk out on him like this? It was as though someone had speared his chest. How was he supposed to function? Grabbing the handle to the front door he wrapped his fist around it, clenching so hard his skin turned white.

Was this how he'd made Maggie feel? The question hit him so hard he physically reeled back, releasing the door. No, what he'd done was worse, far worse. He'd stomped on her feelings and told her he didn't want her. He at least had hope. She might have gone tonight, but that didn't mean he was about to give up. If she'd told him to stay away he would have respected that, but she hadn't. Standing in the doorway to his workspace,

138

he rested his arm on the frame, his eyes drawn to the couch. His mind replayed the images of easing her body down and covering it with his own. He swallowed hard and forced his gaze away. Catching sight of the pages of his work that were strewn on the floor, his heart lurched. That was why he couldn't give up on her. Yes, making love to her had been extraordinary, just as it had been that first time, but it was more than that. Her admiration of his work had felt like more than attraction, it had felt like respect. In that moment, he'd believed he had his friend back. It had felt as though the world had taken a deep breath and settled into its rightful place. Now she was gone. He itched to chase after her, to plead with her, but he knew that turning up at the house and banging to be let in while Evie was asleep wasn't going to do him any favours.

Was he really just going to let her go? Moving to look out the window, Nathan registered his truck sitting in the space that he laughingly called a driveway. Maggie had walked home. The need to know she was safe swept through him. Picking up his phone, he started to swipe through to dial her number, before pausing. He couldn't speak to her over the phone; she deserved to hear all the things he had to say face to face. Instead, he tapped out a text.

I understand if you need some space. Please just let me know you got home okay.

Holding the phone, he stood motionless, silently pleading to whoever might be listening that she would reply. He might have decided to respect her need for space, for tonight at least, but he wasn't going to be able to stick to that resolution if he couldn't be sure she was safe.

It seemed an eternity passed before the little bouncing ellipsis appeared, letting him know she was responding.

I'm home.

Just two words. Well, it wasn't the declaration of love he'd hoped for. If anything, she'd probably only replied out of fear he'd turn up at the cottage if she didn't, but at least she wasn't ignoring him completely. One night, he just needed to get through one night, then he could go and see her.

Pouring a generous serving of whisky, he swallowed it in one go before refilling the glass. It was going to be a long night.

Adjusting his sunglasses against the rare winter sun, Nathan stood across the road from the office of Frederick & Green, waiting for Maggie to arrive. He had been tempted to go to the cottage first thing, but he didn't think Maggie would appreciate him attempting to have this conversation in front of Evie.

Pulling his phone from his back pocket, he glanced at the time again. Susie had been pottering in the office since he'd arrived, almost twenty minutes now, he realised, taking in the fact it was quarter past nine. Even if Maggie had been delayed dropping Evie to school, she'd have been here long before now. He was going to have to go in and ask Susie where Maggie was.

"So, are you coming in, or are you just going to stand there like a weird stalker all day?" Susie's amused tone made Nathan look up from his phone to see her standing outside the office, her head tilted to one side, hands on hips.

He gave her a rueful smile. "I was hoping to catch Maggie," he admitted as he walked over.

No point hiding what she would have already worked out.

Susie's bright smile dimmed slightly, and she folded her arms across her chest. "Not sure why you'd bother, but standing there isn't going to help with that. She's taken a couple of days off."

"What for?" Nathan asked, a spike in concern overriding the half-formed questions that had begun rising at the reminder of Susie's coldness to Maggie. Surely last night hadn't upset her so much that she'd taken time off work.

"You don't think she'd bother explaining to me, do you?" Susie replied, raising her eyebrows.

Well, not while you're being so hostile to her, Nathan thought, keeping the observation to himself. He absentmindedly wondered whether part of Susie's issue was the same problem he'd been dealing with up until a few days ago, namely that she believed Maggie and Dean were in a relationship. He seemed to remember Susie following Dean around all the time when they'd been younger.

"Was it planned?" Nathan asked.

"Yes, she mentioned it a couple of days before the wedding," Susie said with a shrug.

Nathan's shoulders eased down an inch. Whatever she was off for, it wasn't because of him. Thinking back, he realised that it had been a couple of days before the wedding when he'd found Maggie crying in the graveyard.

"Do you want to come in and have a coffee?" Susie asked.

"No, I'd better go, things to do today," Nathan said, knowing he'd be hard pressed to come up with anything he had to do that didn't involve tracking Maggie down if Susie asked him.

"Okay, do you want me to give Maggie a message if I see her?"

If he hadn't been so focused on working out where to check next, Nathan would have smiled at the curiosity in Susie's expression. Shaking his head, he turned and headed in the direction of the cottage.

Having knocked on the front and back doors of the cottage, and peered through the windows like the stalker Susie had accused him of being, Nathan sank against the porch wall, his arse hitting the paving slabs hard enough that he knew it should have hurt. Placing his elbows on his knees, he rubbed his face, the rasp of stubble reminding him that he hadn't bothered to shave that morning. He hadn't been able to concentrate on anything except seeing Maggie, so even if he'd thought of it, the idea of having a sharp blade near his face would not have been a good idea.

She wasn't at work, and despite Sarah's car, which Maggie had been borrowing, being here, she wasn't at home. He didn't have any clue where else to look. When the cold seeping through his jeans finally registered, he realised he couldn't spend the day sitting there. Maybe his mum knew where she was.

Letting himself into his childhood home, Nathan called out. "Mum?"

"I'm in the kitchen, Nathan," Grace called back, no hint of surprise in her voice at him rocking up unexpectedly.

As he walked in, he smiled at the sight of her pulling a loaf tin out of the oven and placing it next to two others on her array of trivets.

"They will be too hot to eat for about twenty minutes, but you can have a slice then if you're still here," she said, slipping her oven gloves off and pulling him in for a hug.

"What brings you here so early? Don't you have work to do?" asked Agnes.

Nathan shifted and grinned at the sight of his gran sitting at the kitchen table. As usual she had her giant mug of tea and a slice of what was obviously the last of Grace's previous batch of baking. Thankfully, the scent filling the kitchen reassured him that it wasn't Agnes's baking that had just been lifted from the oven.

Nathan smiled at his gran's question. She'd decided a couple of years ago that she was old enough to start doing whatever the hell she fancied, and in her book, that had meant not getting up before nine a.m. The thought of his eighty-something-year-old gran rebelling against some imaginary rules by having a lie in every day shook off some of his tension.

"I'd been hoping to see Maggie. She wasn't at work so I checked the cottage, but she wasn't home either," he said, trying to keep his tone relaxed, something that clearly hadn't worked given the knowing look his mum gave him.

"I don't know where she is, but she had to get away early so she asked me to take Evie to school, and for Evie to sleep over here tonight," Grace said, smiling with delight at having her granddaughter. She passed Nathan a mug of tea and gestured for him to sit at the table with them.

"Did you ask her what she's doing?" Agnes asked.

"No, she seemed a bit uncomfortable asking me for help, so I didn't want to pry."

Nathan wanted to groan that his gran hadn't been around when the request had been made; there was no way Maggie would have been able to leave the house without sharing every detail of her plans. Now he had no idea where to start.

"Nonsense, young girl like that needs to tell someone where she's going; we need to know," Agnes said, her expression serious as she picked up her giant mug and slurped loudly.

"We don't need to know, you just *want* to know," Grace said, her tone one of someone who was trying to explain something that she knew would never sink in. "She's lived in London for years, and we don't know what she's doing there most of the time."

Maybe she's gone back to the city? Nathan thought. The idea that Maggie might have gone to visit her ex had him tightening his grip on his mug.

"Fine, I *want* to know. Besides, you never know what can happen. Edna got goosed at the senior gin tasting last weekend," Agnes said, her grin stretching her crepe cheeks as Grace groaned.

Nathan stared at her, mouth open at the thought of his gran's friend Edna, whose back troubles had left her stooped well over a decade ago, having someone's hand up her skirt.

"I wonder if I could get goosed?" Agnes mused, a wistful look on her face.

"You are not to go around trying to get goosed," Grace said sharply.

Suppressing the grin that threatened to spread across his face, Nathan let them continue with their good-natured bickering. With Sarah's Mini sitting outside of the cottage, Maggie couldn't have gone far, unless she'd taken the train somewhere, but surely she'd have driven to the station? He should head home and work on his proposals for Andersson Hotels, but he knew if he tried before he sorted things out with Maggie it would be complete crap. Now he needed to come up with an excuse to hang around long enough for her to return.

"If you're not busy, you could have a look at Evie's bed for me," Grace said, breaking into his thoughts.

"Sure, what's wrong with it?"

"Her bed in the cottage was creaking last time I tucked her in; it makes me nervous."

Nathan smiled; his mum was probably worrying about nothing, but when it came to her only grandchild, she couldn't help herself. Given that the bed was one of those elevated cabin beds with desk space underneath, he didn't think it would hurt to check it out. Besides, it gave him the perfect reason to hang around.

Letting himself into the cottage kitchen with his parents' key felt weird. He'd spent half his childhood in here, but he didn't think he'd ever been alone. Despite the emptiness, the room still had the familiar cosy feel, but the way his steps echoed in the silence as he crossed the room left him with a sense of unease.

Glancing at the whiteboard that Paul and Sarah used to co-ordinate their busy schedules, Nathan smiled at the array of flowers that had been drawn, replacing the usual list of times and places. It looked as though Evie and Maggie had been having fun. Unfortunately, it meant that it didn't give him any clue as to where Maggie had gone, or more importantly, when she'd be back.

Toolbox in hand, Nathan headed upstairs to Evie's room and gave the bed frame a good shake. There was a small creak as he did so, but as he'd expected it was nothing to worry about, just the natural sound of wood shifting. He decided to take the opportunity to check the joints and tighten the screws holding the thing together anyway. His mum would be pleased he'd checked.

Once he'd finished, he leant back on his heels and glanced down the hall. He shouldn't, he really shouldn't, but the sight of Maggie's half-open door was irresistible.

Moving quickly to her room so he didn't have time to change his mind, or start berating himself, Nathan pushed the door fully open. A quick look reassured him that the spotless room had no Maggie in it. A smile curled the edge of his mouth at the memory of just how different it had been when they had been growing up. He'd gone years between seeing her carpet with the amount of stuff that was always spread everywhere.

His smile fell and he pulled the door back into its original, half-open position. What had happened to wind her so tightly? He was seriously starting to worry about where she had gone and whether she was okay.

Back downstairs Nathan grabbed the notepad and pen next to the phone, planning to leave Maggie a note so she'd know he'd been in the house. As he finished, he noticed the blinking light on the voicemail. What if it was urgent? What if it was Evie's school? Okay, he knew that was unlikely, but the knot in his gut tightened.

You're being ridiculous, he chided himself. He couldn't use his concern as an excuse to invade Maggie's privacy any further than he already had. He wouldn't. There had been years where he hadn't known where she was and if she was okay, and now he decided he couldn't cope?

"Staring at that answering machine isn't going to achieve anything."

Nathan swung his head around at the sound of his gran's voice, and he blinked hard, trying to pull his thoughts together enough to answer her.

"Well? Have you fixed my great-grandchild's bed?"

"Yes, it was fine but I've tightened everything up to be sure," Nathan replied, relieved to be in safe conversational territory with the whip-smart woman.

"Good, what you writing there?"

"Just a note for Maggie so she knows about it."

"Good idea, it's no good to go creeping around someone's house." Agnes shuffled next to him and, before Nathan realised what she was doing, she pressed the play button on the answerphone.

"Gran, you can't do that, it's private."

"Tsk, I'm old, I can do what I want," she said over the sound of the machine stating there was one new message.

"Being old isn't some kind of free pass, you know," Nathan said.

"Shhh," Agnes said, rolling her eyes at him. "Do you want to hear the message or not?"

Feeling guilty for doing so, but unable to resist, Nathan quietened down.

"Message left at six-thirty a.m. on Thursday 17th December," the robotic voice announced before being replaced by a real human one.

"Miss Green, it's Elizabeth from the hospital. We forgot to send you a leaflet with your surgery confirmation letter stating that you need to bring any medication you are taking with you today. Can you make sure you bring them, as the surgeon will want to check them before you have the anaesthetic? Sorry for the mix-up, we'll see you soon."

Nathan's blood turned to ice in the space of a single heartbeat. *Surgery? What surgery? What the hell?*

"Did you know she was having surgery today?" he asked, frowning.

"No, and the fact she didn't tell Grace means she didn't want anyone to know," Agnes said, her usually cheerful features puckered with concern. "You'll go and find her?"

"Yes," Nathan said, knowing it hadn't really been a question. Whether Maggie wanted people to know or not, there was no way he was leaving her to face surgery alone.

Turning to leave, Nathan stopped and looked back at Agnes.

"We need to keep this to ourselves," he said. "It's Maggie's business, and I know I'm going to go and find her, but we need to let her tell the family when she's ready."

Agnes nodded, her expression serious for a beat before the familiar twinkle returned. "It'll be our secret," she said.

Oh God, she was going to be a real pain about this, he just knew it. Nathan didn't hold out much hope she'd be able to keep the secret long enough for Maggie to feel ready to share it.

CHAPTER TWENTY-FOUR

Maggie's eyes fluttered open briefly before sinking closed again. What could have been seconds, or hours, later they opened again. She took in the sight of a smiling nurse wearing a set of blue polyester scrubs.

"Welcome back, Maggie," he said, his voice quiet, but relaxed.

Maggie opened her mouth to reply and swallowed against the dryness, her throat aching with the action.

"You can have a sip of water in a moment," the nurse said. "I'll just finish your obs."

Maggie watched the man work efficiently, jotting down her blood pressure and the other bits of information that the machine she was hooked up to seemed to be bleeping out.

"Where am I?" she asked, after taking a grateful sip of the water the nurse had passed her.

"You're on the recovery ward. We just need to make sure you come round fully before you go back to your ward."

Okay, the recovery ward, she'd been expecting that. She figured she should be feeling something, but all that registered was a sense of having woken from the deepest, most rejuvenating sleep she'd ever had. Nothing hurt, a fact for which she was extremely grateful.

"Everything went to plan. Dr Brook will come and see you on the ward later so he can talk to you in detail," the nurse said with smile, gently patting her arm before heading away.

Maggie closed her eyes; she'd care about the outcome later. Right now, she couldn't seem to make her brain connect her thoughts together.

Being pushed through the corridors on a bed a short while later was a strange experience, but Maggie was just grateful that she had obviously recovered enough from the surgery and anaesthetic that they felt able to release her back on to the normal ward.

She was pushed around the corner into a space that held four beds.

She let the porter push her into position and answered the new nurse's questions. It was over; now all she had to do was get through the follow up appointment and hope like hell they had been able to remove everything. Mr Brook's words from the pre-consultation that morning rang through her head: *Adenocarcinoma* — she had no idea why it was significant that it was that type of cancer.

Maggie shifted to pour some of the water that had been left in a plastic jug next to her bed into the small cup, silently thanking whatever drugs she had been given for the fact she still couldn't feel anything. She had a horrible feeling it wasn't going to last, but for now she felt good. Weirdly so, considering, and she had the added plus of only having to avoid calls from work now that she'd faced up to this. They, unfortunately, hadn't stopped calling her. Not that she bothered listening to any of the messages.

After taking a sip of the water, she tilted her head back to rest on the stack of pillows and closed her eyes.

"Oh my God, Maggie."

Her head snapped up at the sound of that voice, a voice she would know anywhere. How was he here? He shouldn't be here.

Meeting Nathan's gaze, she took in his tight, drawn expression, the pale, almost grey sheen to his complexion. He looked like he had been the one having an operation. The thought made her smile.

"You're okay?" he asked, his features loosening slightly.

"How are you here?" Maggie asked.

"I had to talk to you after last night," he said.

"Seems a bit extreme to track me down to here," she said, trying to work out how he'd found her.

"What's wrong?" he asked.

And there it was, the question she hadn't wanted to answer to anyone. The reason she'd come alone. She frowned, struggling to pull her thoughts together enough to figure out how to answer him.

He moved to the side of the bed and took her hand in his, careful to avoid the cannula that had been left in place as a precaution. The sight of him standing there, concern etched into his expression, made her heart soar. *No*, she reminded herself. That was a dangerous reaction; she couldn't afford to rely on him. She'd got through this morning, but she still had no idea what that meant for her future, or whether she even had one, but she did know she had to depend on herself.

"Maggie, please, you need to tell me what's going on. My heart about stopped when I realised you were here, that you were having an operation."

"I'm okay, it all went fine," Maggie said, not really knowing how else to respond, but wanting to reassure him. She needed to take control before he tried to, before she admitted she wanted him to.

"Maggie, you're in a hospital, you've had surgery. You are not okay."

"Well, I wasn't, but I am now," she said. "You really don't need to be here."

Nathan flinched at her words, and a small part of her wished she could take them back, but a bigger part knew it would be better for them both if he left.

"Miss Green, how are you feeling?" Dr Brooks asked, stopping her before she could make things worse.

"I feel pretty good. I thought I'd be in pain," Maggie said, turning her attention to her consultant.

"They have you on some pretty good stuff," he said with a gentle smile. "We had to take quite a lot of tissue, so you're likely to feel uncomfortable for a couple of days. You'll need to keep dosed up on paracetamol once the pain relief you've had intravenously starts to wear off."

"Did it go okay?" she asked.

"Yes, everything went as planned; we did have to take more tissue than I'd initially thought, but otherwise everything went well."

"Did you get it all?" she asked, barely noticing that she had tightened her grip on Nathan's hand.

"I won't know for sure until the lab tests are completed, but things look positive." He gave her a kind smile.

Maggie sagged back slightly. She wasn't in the clear yet, but it sounded like things could have been worse.

"Just a reminder that you should rest up for a few days. You're likely to bleed for anything up to two weeks, so that's normal. However, if the bleeding gets heavy then call the reception here immediately."

"Thank you," she said.

"You also need to refrain from intercourse for the next four weeks," he said, giving Nathan a pointed look.

Maggie's gaze moved from her consultant to Nathan, realising she was still holding his hand she pulled away, ignoring the way Nathan's attention shifted from Dr Brooks to where his hand now hung, empty.

"When can I leave?" she asked, crossing her arms over her chest and studiously ignoring Nathan.

"The nurses will make sure that your vitals are stable for another couple of hours. Assuming you manage to pass water in that time, then you will be able to leave."

As Dr Brooks walked away, Maggie closed her eyes. She didn't want to have this conversation.

"I'm not going to push you," Nathan said quietly. "But, you are going to have to tell me at some point."

Maggie eased her eyes open and peered at Nathan through the small slit. She nodded her agreement. As long as she didn't have to explain right now, she'd agree to anything.

Sinking into the chair next to her, Nathan dragged his hands down his face, the rasp of his fair stubble audible against the backdrop of beeps and buzzes from the equipment around them.

"Just tell me one thing," he said.

Maggie looked at him cautiously.

"Are you dying?"

She felt as though every cell in her body froze instantly. How the hell was she supposed to answer that when she didn't know for certain herself? "I don't think so," she said, her words barely a whisper.

His already pale features seemed to fade even further at her response, but he didn't speak, instead he moved so he was sitting on the edge of her bed and gently pulled her into his arms. "I love you, Maggie. I'm here for you no matter what this is, no matter what you need. You won't have to face it alone."

Maggie let herself sink into his arms, the comfort of being wrapped up in Nathan tearing down the wall she'd had in place since that awful phone call. Tears streamed down her face as her thoughts ran wild with all the fears she had been fighting so hard to supress. Having the fact she had cancer confirmed that morning had barely had time to sink in before she'd been walking down to theatre. It shouldn't have been a shock, but she'd been trying so hard to avoid thinking about the possibility that having it confirmed had been like a cold hard slap.

Nathan's hand ran up and down her back as he cradled her head against him. Her tears had become sobs before she was finally able to begin reeling her emotions back into place. Leaning back, she smiled awkwardly at him.

"Sorry," she said.

"Don't you dare apologise for leaning on me. I love you."

Heart pounding, Maggie realised she wanted nothing more than to lean closer, to kiss him, to lean on him and have his support for whatever came next. The need to have him at her side swept over her in a wave of longing so strong that she had to suck in a breath to hold her tongue. The fact he was here, freely offering what she'd always wanted, bloomed a happiness that she wouldn't have believed possible. Hot on its heels came that warning voice. She'd let herself need Nathan once before. She'd barely survived that heartbreak; she didn't think she could take it a second time, especially not on top of everything else. She couldn't lean on him, she couldn't depend on anyone except herself.

Shaking her head, she pulled back.

Nathan's grip tightened. "Don't," he said softly, the single word a plea.

"We aren't a good idea."

"Why, Maggie?"

"I wasn't enough for you when I was eighteen. I'm certainly not going to be enough for you now."

"What do you mean? You're all I want, you're all I need," he said, finally allowing her to pull back.

Maggie just looked at him.

"Are you trying to punish me for letting you go all those years ago? You should know you don't need to. I'm punishing myself enough. My life has been empty without you in it. I spent years travelling, just to try and find a way to fill the void you left inside me."

"Letting me go?" Maggie said, her grief at knowing she couldn't give in shoved firmly aside by what he was saying. "You didn't *let* me go, you left me. I might have been the one that got on that train, but it was you who stood on that platform and pushed."

Pain flared in his eyes at her words, but all she felt was a glimmer of satisfaction that, maybe, he was finally getting it. He slipped off the bed and back onto the hard plastic chair next to her, burying his face in his hands. He was silent for so long she had decided he wasn't going to reply when he finally spoke.

"I thought I was doing what was best for you, Maggie, but I know I can't justify what I did. That doesn't mean I'm not going to be here for you now."

She didn't want to hear his excuses, but a little bit of her sagged at the realisation he really wasn't going to fight for her. "You don't need to be here. I'll be going back to the cottage later."

"And how are you getting there? Sarah's car is at the cottage, so I'm assuming you shouldn't be driving." Nathan looked at her, his expression expectant.

"I have a taxi booked to take me to the train station."

"Not a chance in hell, Maggie. I'm staying here for as long as you are. I'm taking you home, and I'm taking care of you once you're there." He crossed his arms, the set of his jaw making it clear he expected her to go along with his declaration.

Maggie's eyes filled and she squeezed them closed, desperate to hold on to her composure after her earlier meltdown. "I don't want you here," she said, the lie slipping past her lips more easily than she had expected.

"Well, I'm not going anywhere."

She couldn't have him here, she was too vulnerable, too likely to slip and fall for his fickle promises. He had to leave. "Don't you get it?" she asked, forcing her tone into the no-nonsense one she used on difficult clients. "Your words don't mean anything. Your promises don't mean anything. I don't trust you. You taught me that I can't rely on you, so why would I want you here now?"

Maggie paused, watching the play of emotions across Nathan's face, the sharp flinch as her words hit him. She told herself it was what she wanted. She needed to hurt him. He had to leave, and this was the only way she knew how to make that happen. Chest heaving, she braced herself for his departure.

"Gran knows you're here," Nathan said. "Do you think I'd survive her finding out I'd left you to make your own way home?"

Sinking back into the bed, Maggie breathed out a sigh. She knew when she was beat.

CHAPTER TWENTY-FIVE

Easing out of the car, Maggie had no choice but to let Nathan support her to the cottage. Shivering, she kept on eye on his parents' farmhouse; knowing that they would only want to help didn't make her ready to deal with all of the Parkers.

"Don't worry, I've asked Gran to run interference so no one sees you arriving back," Nathan said, as if reading her mind.

"I don't want you to have to lie to them," Maggie said, knowing how hard that would be for him, and not really wanting to lie to them herself.

"I'm not going to lie to anyone, but you want space to deal with this yourself before you have to deal with anyone else, and I'm going to make sure you get it," he said, and the part of her heart that wished she really could lean on him, and not just for this moment, swelled.

"Do you need the bathroom or shall we get you straight into your bed?"

"Bed sounds good," she said. She didn't know how she could feel so tired when she had been asleep for half the morning, but the journey seemed to have zapped her energy.

"I like the sound of that."

"What?" she asked, confused.

"You asking me to take you to bed."

Maggie felt her mouth form an O as she registered Nathan's words. Looking up, she met eyes glinting with amusement.

Once in her room, she had to almost physically eject him so she could pull a nightshirt on and slip between the sheets. He insisted on standing at the doorway, his back to her, but she didn't have the energy to fight him any further.

"I'm decent," she said, once she was safely in bed, her covers pulled up to her chin. Why was she so cold?

"You look so pale," Nathan said, his hand stroking across her temple after he'd grabbed a blanket from the top of her wardrobe. He gently brushed her hair back from her face in the way she could remember her mother doing for her when she'd been ill as a child. The contact soothed, and despite her best intentions, Maggie realised she was glad he was there.

"Thank you," she said softly.

"For what?" he asked, his brow wrinkling.

"For bringing me home," she explained, her eyes drifting closed. She knew she could have made it on the train, but it would have been much harder.

"I'll be here for you as much as you'll let me," he said, the words barely registering as she drifted off.

"Maggie, princess, I just need you to take these." A deep voice seemed to rumble through Maggie, heating her body as she was dragged back to consciousness.

As her eyes opened, the heat that had been building was instantly washed away with a deep, aching pain. Giving a low moan, she curled her legs up and wrapped her arms around her abdomen.

"I know, princess, but if you take these you'll feel better soon."

Maggie blinked and took in the sight of Nathan. He still had on the pale blue T-shirt he'd been wearing last time she saw him, although it was a lot more rumpled. He was wearing jeans, but his feet were bare. His usually tousled hair looked as though he'd just crawled out of bed.

Why was he here? As she came around more fully, her brain caught up with her, and a quick glance at the clock told her it was two a.m.

"What are you doing back here?" Maggie asked, the words coming out on a croak as she cleared her throat.

"I didn't leave," Nathan said with a gentle smile. It wasn't the amused one she loved so much, but the scar on his chin shifted, drawing her attention to his face, to his lips. "I'm sorry to wake you up, but it's time for you to take these painkillers. They'll make you feel better soon."

Maggie shifted onto her side and eased herself up. Nathan's hand curled around her shoulder, helping to take some of her weight so she didn't have to use her core. Once she was upright, she gratefully took the tablets from Nathan's palm and swallowed them with a mouthful of water.

"How bad do you feel? The hospital said you can have ibuprofen as well as paracetamol if you need it."

Taking a moment to let herself register the sensations in her body, Maggie shook her head. "It's not that bad," she said. "Just like strong stomach cramps really."

"Please take them if you think it'd help. I don't want you to suffer."

Maggie summoned up a smile. "Honestly, I'm okay. You don't need to stay," she said, her eyes heavy as she moved to lie back down.

Nathan helped her reposition her pillows once she was lying down. "I'm not going anywhere," he said, placing a gentle kiss on her forehead, before flicking the lamp back off and creeping back out of the room.

Some part of her wondered where he was sleeping, but before she could explore the thought, and the pang of regret that it wasn't at her side, sleep claimed her again.

Blinking, Maggie studied the Echo Dot on her bedside table, which let her know it was almost eleven a.m. She resisted the urge to leap out of bed in a panic. She'd been advised the anaesthetic might make her sleepy for a few days, so she was extremely grateful that she'd arranged for Grace and Arthur to have Evie overnight, and get her to school today. At least after today it was the weekend, so there was no schedule to stick to.

As she swung her legs over the side of the bed, the deep ache in her abdomen hit her and she let out a small groan. Sucking in a breath, Maggie held still, waiting for her body to catch up with her. Once the initial wave of discomfort had passed, she registered the sight of a glass of water and tablets on the side. *Nathan.* The memory of him waking her in the night to make sure she took her painkillers flashed into her mind. He'd stayed. *Only for now*, the voice in her head warned, but the warmth of knowing he had stayed didn't leave her.

Her stomach twisted at the realisation that, other than a few bites of the sandwich the nurses had insisted she have before leaving the hospital, she hadn't eaten anything since Wednesday. She stood slowly. Making her way downstairs, she knew she was being overcautious with her movements, but she didn't want to risk another jolt of pain like the one when she'd tried to get out of bed.

A strange scratching sound greeted her as she approached the kitchen. Feeling strangely lightheaded, Maggie paused, tilting her head to one side to try to identify the sound before shuffling forward.

Reaching the kitchen doorway, she took in the solid curve of Nathan's spine. Sitting at the kitchen table, he was leaning over, his hand moving rapidly over the sheet of paper, his focus absolute. She didn't want to disturb his concentration, but she knew she needed to sit for a few moments to regain her strength before sorting out a snack.

Moving next to him, Maggie smiled as he jerked up at her presence. The small buds he had in his ears made the reason he hadn't heard her approach clear. Tapping on his phone, Nathan silenced the music and slipped the buds out of his ears.

"I didn't realise you were awake," he said, studying her carefully. "You should have called me."

"I didn't think you'd still be here," Maggie said honestly, the double meaning behind her words only occurring to her as she took in the slight pinch that flickered around his eyes.

"I'm not going anywhere," Nathan said, his tone firm, determined.

Taking a deep breath, Maggie didn't bother responding. She didn't have the energy to argue with him, and he was going to go at some point. She just needed to be strong enough not to get used to his presence for as long as it took for that to happen.

"Well, if you're sticking around, you can make me a cup of tea and some toast," she said, turning her attention from those brilliant blue eyes to his drawings.

"Nice to see you being more like yourself," Nathan said as he rose without argument.

"What do you mean?"

"Ordering me around," he said with a smile, as he moved efficiently around the kitchen space, pulling items out of the cupboards and fridge. "The Maggie I remember was outspoken and good at getting her own way. You seemed too quick to just go along with what other people wanted when you came back."

"Like when?"

"Like going to a vegan restaurant with Sarah."

Maggie thought about it and realised Nathan was right; when they'd been friends, she would never have gone somewhere she didn't fancy. Had she really lost so much of herself?

"Are these more drawings for Andersson Hotels?" she asked, turning her attention to the beautiful images on the table.

"Yes, I feel like they are missing something, but they're getting there."

Studying the huge sheets of paper that covered the table, Maggie took in the bold strokes, the perfectly crafted lines that displayed the juxtaposition of intricate detail against solid, natural-looking elements. She was coming to realise that that blend was the hallmark of Nathan's work. She couldn't see that they were anything less than perfect already.

"I can't imagine how you would make these any better; they are extraordinary," she said, turning to smile at him. "I guess that's why you're the artist and I'm the accountant."

Nathan's eyes lit up at her words. "Do you really think so?"

"I'm pretty sure I'm an accountant, so yes," Maggie teased, feeling lighter than she had in weeks. She hadn't realised how much of her own character she'd been suppressing in her efforts to be perfect. Being with Nathan, teasing him, holding her own with him, she felt like herself in a way she hadn't realised she'd been missing.

"You know what I mean," he said, leaning his tall frame against the kitchen unit and crossing his arms over his chest as he looked at her levelly.

"Yes, you are incredibly talented," she said, her eyes flickering away from the intensity in his gaze.

"Thank you," he said, his voice thick with unexpected emotion.

CHAPTER TWENTY-SIX

"I know you have better things to do than to keep hanging around here," Maggie said, the following evening.

Nathan looked at her over the top of Evie's bowed head. "There is nothing better than hanging around with you." He glanced down at Evie's suddenly upturned face and amended, "With both of you."

He supressed a smile at the flare of emotion that greeted him from Maggie's deep brown eyes. He was slowly breaking down those defences. When she had told him her diagnosis, his heart had just about pounded out of his chest. Her courage was incredible and only made him love her more. He couldn't pretend he wasn't terrified for her, but that didn't mean he didn't want to be a part of her life, for as long as possible.

"Don't you have to finish preparing for your Andersson meeting?"

"You don't need to worry about that, it's all in hand."

"But it's a big opportunity for you to kit out their new Bristol hotel."

Nathan smiled; if Maggie had any idea how big, she'd never let him stay. Besides, there was a small part of him that didn't want to let her know that he could be in line for a contract for all of their hotels, not just their Bristol one. If he did persuade her to take him back, he wanted it to be because of him, not because of some potential success that might not even come to anything. He wasn't like the city boy bankers she was used to, he certainly wasn't ever going to have the sort of money they had, and he wanted any relationship they developed to be about him, not his job.

"I'm pretty much ready," Nathan said as he mentally ticked through his list. He had a few final bits to complete, but given that Sarah and Paul were back early tomorrow, and he wouldn't get away with hanging around Maggie all the time, he'd have time to complete everything ahead of his Christmas Eve meeting with Andersson Hotels.

More importantly, that meant he only had today, and this evening, before his almost permanent presence in the cottage would have to come to an end. Less than twelve hours before his efforts to prove to Maggie they should give their future a try would become much more difficult.

"You know I'm fine now, though," Maggie said.

Nathan smiled at her, lifting his mug to his lips without comment. He knew she was fine, physically at least, but that didn't mean he was about to give up what little time he had left to hang around unquestioned.

"What are we going to do today?" Evie asked, eyes bright as she looked between the two of them.

"What would you like to do, pumpkin?" Maggie asked.

"I know what I'd like to do," Nathan said, giving Maggie a half smile as he stretched his arm around Evie's back and traced his finger down Maggie's arm.

"Well, given my recent appointment, that's definitely not on the cards," Maggie said, eyebrows raised.

"I know, I was just sharing my thoughts," he said with a shrug, his lips curling as he enjoyed the pink tinge that had spread across Maggie's cheeks.

She wasn't as unaffected by the suggestion as she wanted him to believe. He paused for a minute, unable to resist adding, "So it would have been on the cards otherwise?"

Maggie swatted his arm away, but the twinkle in her eyes let him know he wasn't completely wrong.

"What do you want to do, Uncle Nathan?" Evie looked up at him, her blue eyes wide with curiosity.

Maggie laughed silently at what he was sure was an expression of horror on his face. He definitely wasn't explaining that train of thought to his ten-year-old niece.

"Why don't we go to the park?" Maggie suggested, rescuing him from trying to explain himself.

"Oh yes," Evie said, pushing her chair back from the table and dropping her pencils. "I'll get my shoes on."

"Looks like we're going right this moment," Nathan said.

"Can you change into your warm jeans and get a big jumper as well first?" Maggie shouted to the retreating Evie. "Thank you for your help over the last few days," she said to Nathan, her eyes glistening slightly as she spoke. "I know I wasn't very appreciative of you being around to start with, but I really am very grateful."

Without breaking contact with her deep brown eyes, Nathan moved into Evie's chair so he was right next to Maggie. Taking her hand in his, he smiled gently. "I'm sorry I let you down when we were younger. I really thought I was doing the best thing for you. I was an idiot, and you need to know that I will never let you down again. I know you're worried about what the future holds, but I will always be here for you. I will always give you anything and everything you need. I will give you everything I have and everything I am. I love you."

Maggie blinked at him, her body leaning towards him almost imperceptibly before freezing.

Nathan slowly lifted his hand, gently cupping her cheek. The sensation of her soft, warm skin made him want to pull her against him and hold her in his arms forever. "Please forgive me. Please give us another chance."

For a brief moment her expression softened, and the hope and need he was sure covered his own features was reflected back at him, but almost as quickly, it vanished. Maggie unfroze, unfortunately not in the direction he wanted her to. She pulled back, slipping out of her chair and staring at him, eyes wide.

She opened her mouth to reply, but someone banged on the door and her head turned towards the source of the sound.

"I'll get it," Evie shouted, as her feet thundered down the stairs.

"I, um, I should," Maggie said, gesturing to the door.

Nathan's hand shot out and grabbed her wrist. "Please," he whispered, not really knowing what he was specifically asking for at that instant, but needing something from her.

Maggie shook her head, her expression conflicted, and pulled her hand out of his grasp. "I'd better go and see who that is," she said.

Nathan followed her, knowing he should be more curious about who was at the door; after all, just about everyone who came here would just walk in. Instead, he couldn't help but worry that he'd never find the words to get her to forgive him, and even if they couldn't be together, he needed her forgiveness. It was the only way he was going to be able to close that hole deep inside.

Following Maggie, Nathan was so wrapped up in his own thoughts that he didn't pay much attention to the figure standing in the doorway, until her cold tone slipped through to his consciousness. "What are you doing here?"

"You weren't answering my calls," a cultured male voice said.

Nathan's head snapped, his body tensing at the sight of a man in an immaculately tailored woollen coat. Jet black hair was smoothed back from his forehead, not a single strand out of place. He had that slight pretty boy look, and posture, that screamed private school. What bothered Nathan the most, though, was the almost proprietary way he was looking at Maggie. Who the hell was he?

"That should have been clue enough," Maggie replied, and Nathan took a step forward, shifting so that he was right behind her. If it hadn't been for the narrow hallway, he'd have moved so she was sheltered behind him.

"You need to be reasonable, Maggie. You have to hear me out."

"I really don't have to be anything, Rupert," she said. "You gave up the right to expect anything from me when you ended things."

At the name Nathan did move, and without considering the fact he was likely to look ridiculous, he shuffled to the side and past Maggie. Thanks to Dean, he knew exactly who Rupert was, and he didn't want the man anywhere near Maggie.

"She doesn't want to talk to you, so I suggest you leave," Nathan said, his arms crossed over his chest.

The man looked him up and down, judgement clear in his eyes as he took in Nathan's worn jeans and a T-shirt stained with a myriad of wood treatments. When he took in Nathan's bare feet, he snorted. Meeting Nathan's eyes again, he smiled. "With hair like that, you must be one of Dean Parker's brothers," Rupert said, the words clearly meant to be an insult.

"Who I am is irrelevant. Maggie doesn't want to speak to you, so you need to leave."

"Maggie, are you really going to let this … this Neanderthal tell you what to do? I've come all this way; we need to talk."

Nathan lifted his hand to the door, ready to swing it closed; he wasn't about to let this arse continue taking up their time, especially when he had so precious little of it left before he would have to share Maggie with her sister again.

"Fine, you should come in," Maggie said, her tone resigned.

Turning slightly, Nathan looked at her. "You really don't have to speak to him."

"I know, but I want to," she said, her face pale but determined.

Nathan's heart sank. She wanted to speak to him? He didn't want her to want to speak to the man. He wanted her to be focused on him, on them. He opened his mouth to protest but closed it again. The only thing he had the right to do at this moment was to respect her wishes. He certainly wasn't going to start calling the shots. He'd leave that sort of behaviour to people like Rupert. Instead he nodded, his jaw tight.

"Would you mind taking Evie to the park?" Maggie asked, and Nathan's heart sank further.

He didn't want to leave her alone with this guy. Nathan might act it occasionally, but he wasn't stupid, and there was only one reason a man like Rupert travelled all this way, three days before Christmas, and it wasn't to have a casual chat. It certainly didn't help that the man looked like he'd stepped out of the pages of a magazine. Rupert might have hurt Maggie before, but so had Nathan. He'd been asking Maggie to forgive the hurt he'd caused all those years ago, but would she forgive Rupert instead?

"Are you sure you want me to leave you alone with him?" Nathan asked, his words a whisper, for Maggie's ears only. Heart pounding, he silently pleaded for her to say no.

"Yes, he won't hurt me," she replied.

Nodding his agreement, despite every cell in his body wanting to refuse, Nathan slipped his socks and boots on, pulled on his coat as Maggie bundled Evie into hers, and walked out the door, leaving his exposed heart in Maggie's hands.

CHAPTER TWENTY-SEVEN

Maggie led Rupert through to the kitchen, her heart thundering as she flicked the kettle on.

Standing awkwardly, he swivelled his head around, taking it all in. Maggie tried to picture how it would all look to Rupert. It couldn't be any more different to the life they had both lived in London. Here there were no clean lines. Instead of the perfect, high gloss cabinets they had in their respective apartments, there were mismatched oak doors. There were no artfully placed ornaments, giving the barest of nods to the festive season. Instead the ceiling was covered with the paper chains that she and Evie had made. Colour co-ordination definitely wasn't a thing here.

Rupert's face twisted slightly, as though the sight was almost painful, before he schooled his features and faced her again. "You look well," he said.

Maggie laughed at the irony of that. She was dealing with a potentially life-threatening health condition, and he thought she looked well.

"I don't think I've ever seen you in jeans before," he added, his expression shifting to one of very male appreciation.

"You made your opinion of jeans very well known," Maggie said.

"Yes, well, they aren't appropriate for people of our standing, but, well, they certainly suit you."

"This is my standing," she said, gesturing to the room around her with a sweep of her arm. She'd hidden this from him for so long, but found it irritating that he was acting as though she was totally separate from this part of her life, as though finding her here was just a minor inconvenience that would soon be remedied.

Rupert opened and closed his mouth, as though flapping around for something to say.

"Never mind," Maggie said suddenly. "Coffee? It's only instant."

"Um, yes, that would be fine," he said.

"Sit down," she said, pointing him to the table as she busied herself making their drinks.

Maggie guessed that if Rupert hadn't broken up with her, he'd have had to come here eventually. It wasn't as though she could have married the man without him meeting her family, but as she placed a mug of coffee in front of him and took a seat on the opposite side of the table, she realised that she had never once imagined him sitting here, being here. The sight of him as he elegantly crossed his legs, his carefully folded coat on the back of the chair next to him, seemed entirely out of place.

"What did you want to talk about?" Maggie asked, pushing Evie's colouring aside to make space for her own mug.

"You've been ignoring my calls."

"Yes, we've established that. Shall we move on to what you wanted to speak to me about?"

"I made a mistake," Rupert said, picking at an imaginary fleck on his trousers as he spoke.

Despite herself, Maggie smiled. She could only imagine exactly how uncomfortable that little admission had made Rupert. He didn't do mistakes. She stayed silent, waiting for him to elaborate.

"I miss you," he said, looking up to meet her gaze.

The words slipped straight past her brain and into her heart, soothing the bruise that remained from their unexpected break-up. Surprisingly, given how much she'd wanted to hear those very words from him when he'd dumped her, they didn't make her as happy as she'd have expected. Was there something so wrong with her that men felt they could drop her and pick her back up when it suited them? It felt like all she did now was listen to men apologise. Although, to be fair, Rupert hadn't actually apologised.

Maggie didn't speak; she simply lifted her mug and took a sip of the still too hot tea. The sharp heat was a welcome distraction.

"Maggie, I want us to get back together," Rupert elaborated in the face of her silence.

"Why? A few weeks ago you felt the fact I wasn't going to be at the firm anymore was a good enough reason for us not to be together. That hasn't changed."

"I take it you haven't listened to any of the voicemails they have been leaving you?" he asked.

"I've been deleting all my voicemails," Maggie admitted with a shrug.

"Well, I have good news for you. I've persuaded them that they need you as well as me. They want to talk to you about reinstatement." Rupert leant back in his chair, placing his hands on his knee once he'd finished speaking, a pleased smile on his face.

"I have my job back?" Maggie asked, the words spilling out. To have her job back, to have the security of that wrapped around her again, that would be amazing, wouldn't it? "Why?" she asked, the question slipping out before she could stop it.

Rupert smiled at her, the practised, assured smile he used on his clients. "Two of your biggest clients threatened to walk if they couldn't have you back. The firm soon realised how much they needed you. They know no one is as good as us when we are together."

Maggie smiled, but it felt artificial. Had it really taken such a drastic step for them to value her? She should be delighted, jumping up and down with relief, but something didn't feel quite right. She was being expected to accept the lack of value and respect they had shown, simply because they had worked out that she was worth more to them than they had initially realised. "I don't know," she said slowly.

"You'll be a director," Rupert said. "That's what they are offering, straight into a director role."

Maggie's heart leapt at the thought. She'd worked so hard for it, to become the youngest director in the firm's history, yet, now it was here, hers to take, she wasn't sure. The events of the last few weeks had shown her that she had been far more committed to the company than they had been to her. However, the status, money and achievement? It was everything she'd been dreaming of, wasn't it? As she pictured the corner office that she knew would be hers if she returned, the unparalleled view of the city shimmered, Nathan's face taking its place, his expression open, pleading. She now found herself having to choose between the future she'd been working for, and the future she'd dreamed of as a child. The future that she'd given up on when her battered heart had decided it could take no more.

As Rupert took her hand, she blinked; she hadn't been aware of him moving around the table.

"You and I belong together; we make an amazing team," he said, the soft pad of his manicured thumb gently stroking the back of her hand.

He was right; they did make a good team. He was a couple of years older than her, but they had risen through the ranks together. They had pulled off deals that no one had expected to succeed, and they had driven each other to be better.

Rupert continued to talk, reminding her of the things they had achieved together, reminding her of how compatible they were in every part of their lives.

Maggie stared at their joined hands. His touch didn't make her pulse race, his words didn't make her heart soar, but maybe that was better. The uncontrollable reactions she had to Nathan weren't the sensible choice, they were the stuff of teenage hormones. They were the stuff of heartbreak.

"Maggie, I didn't want to do this here, I wanted to do it somewhere special, somewhere that gave us a spectacular story we could tell for the rest of our lives, but I want to marry you."

Her head jerked up at his words.

Rupert stared at her, his expression careful, as though watching a wild animal, unsure of what reaction to expect.

"What?" she asked, stunned.

Slipping his hand into the pocket of his blazer, he took out a pale turquoise box and placed it on the table in front of her. When she didn't move, he released her hand and pressed the small silver button on the front of the box, easing it open. Inside the box sat an enormous emerald cut diamond solitaire surrounded by a pave diamond band.

"I'm not proposing now, but I'm showing this to you this so you know I mean it. I want to marry you. I want us to have a life together."

"I don't know," Maggie whispered.

"You don't know?" Rupert said flatly. "I've come all this way and bought you one of the most expensive rings Tiffany's had to offer, and you don't know?"

Frowning at the abrupt change in his tone, Maggie turned to face Rupert, shifting her chair to put some distance between them. He was talking to her as if she was a client who was acting unreasonably.

"Rupert, you dumped me because we weren't going to work together anymore, and after a couple of attempts to phone me, you rock up here and expect me to what? Be happy that things can just go back to how they were?"

"Not how they were, better. We can get married; we'll both be directors. That's everything we wanted."

Maggie frowned at him; he was right, it was everything they had talked about, but did she want it anymore? "There's something you should know," she said, knowing that she couldn't consider this option until she knew whether it was still on the table once he knew what she was facing.

"Is it about that guy that was here? Look, I'm not saying I'd be happy if something happened between you two, but we weren't together."

"No, it's not about him," Maggie said, although she had a feeling that, whatever he said, she'd never be able to admit to Rupert that she and Nathan had slept together if she chose to go down this road with him.

"Well, what then?"

"I have cancer," she said.

"What?" he asked, frowning.

"I have cancer. I had an operation a few days ago. I'm waiting to hear if it was successful or not."

"So you'll be fine, then, if you've had surgery," Rupert said, frowning as though confused about why she was raising it.

"I might be, but if I need more treatment that could mean I can't have children, and that's assuming I make it through this."

Rupert studied her for a moment, his face the blank canvas she was used to seeing whenever he was working through a particularly knotty problem. "Well, we always said we weren't bothered about children anyway," he said.

Maggie's heart pinched; this whole conversation seemed to be Rupert reminding her of things she wasn't really sure were true, not anymore.

"Look, I'm here for you; this doesn't change anything for me," he said earnestly.

"I need to think about it," Maggie said, suddenly feeling exhausted.

"Well, why don't I make us a fresh drink while you consider?"

"I'm going to need more than the time it takes to make a cuppa," she said, smiling to try to soften her words.

"Shall I stay here tonight?"

"No, I need space to think. Besides, my sister will be arriving home from her honeymoon in the early hours."

"Oh, I'd forgotten about her," Rupert said. "Well, how long are you going to need?"

"A couple of days?" Maggie suggested, not really sure she that could put a timescale on something so important.

"I don't like it, Maggie. What more do you want from me? I'm offering you everything you wanted. You should be jumping into my arms," Rupert said, as though genuinely confused that he wasn't getting the response he wanted.

"I know and I'm really sorry, I just … it's just that you really hurt me. I can't turn that off like a switch. I need time to process things."

"What about going back to work?"

"I don't know," Maggie said honestly. "I guess I should speak to them before I make a decision."

Rupert paled at her words, and her chest tightened at upsetting him further. "So, you'll put some effort into a decision about your job, but I'm expected to wait? You could at least decide about us before you speak to work. I guess I know where I sit in your priorities," he said, his hands running through his hair, leaving it uncharacteristically messy.

Maggie flinched at the harshness in his voice. "I'm sorry, I didn't mean to make you feel like work was more important than you."

"Well, you need to decide about us first. Don't speak to anyone in the office until you've done that. You owe me that much."

She bristled at him telling her she owed him, but she didn't have the energy to argue. Resisting the urge to bite back, she just nodded.

"That way, maybe we can talk to work together. I can help you decide?" Rupert suggested, his tone more conciliatory.

"I just need some time and space," Maggie said.

"I'm leaving this here so you know exactly what I'm offering you. I'm not giving up," Rupert said, placing the robin-egg blue box back on the table, before pulling his coat back on.

His words made Maggie smile as she watched him walk back up the footpath and climb into his Mercedes. Of course he wasn't giving up. He never did. As she watched him pull away from the kerb, their conversation ran through her mind. Her smile faded at the realisation he hadn't once asked how she was feeling.

CHAPTER TWENTY-EIGHT

"You can play on your computer for an hour if you want," Maggie said to Evie, when Nathan finally brought his niece home.

They'd been at the park for nearly two hours, and they had been the longest two hours of his life.

Nathan's relief at the fact Rupert was gone was short-lived as he took in Maggie's serious expression. It was clear that, even if Rupert wasn't there, Nathan wasn't about to be welcomed with open arms.

"Thanks for taking Evie out," Maggie said, her hand resting on the door, making it clear that she didn't want him to stick around.

"What happened with Rupert?" Nathan asked, unable to stop the question from slipping out, despite knowing he didn't have any right to ask.

"It doesn't matter," Maggie replied, studying his feet as she refused to meet his gaze.

"It matters to me."

His statement made her look up at him, her expression closed. "I need to go and sort dinner for Evie," she said, her words flat as she gestured for him to leave with her head.

"We need to talk," Nathan said, the stone that had been in his stomach for the last couple of hours swelling. What the hell had that man said to her, that Nathan and Maggie had gone from a place where Nathan had felt able to confess his feelings to her, to a place where she wouldn't even look at him? "We need to finish our conversation," he added, not willing to leave until she'd heard him out.

"There's nothing to say."

"I love you; I want us to have a future together. There's plenty to say," Nathan said, trying to make her understand how much she meant to him.

"We don't have a future together," Maggie said, her gaze slipping from his and returning to his shoes.

"We could have."

"No, we couldn't. I can't keep having this same conversation with you, Nathan. I wasn't enough for you then. You know what I'm going through; I'm definitely not going to be enough for you now. I don't even know if I have a future," Maggie said, her voice breaking.

Nathan took a step closer to her. His hand reached for her face, lifting her chin so she would have to face him. "You have always been enough for me. I was afraid I wasn't good enough for you, that you'd resent me for making you stay here, so I did something stupid, I gave you up. I have regretted it every minute of every day since then." He held her gaze as he spoke, needing her to understand, needing her forgiveness. "Please, please give me a second chance."

"I can't," she said, her voice thick.

"Is it him?" he asked, not knowing if he could bear it if she was going to give someone a second chance, just not him.

"I need to think," she said.

He'd left it too late — no, he couldn't have. Nathan didn't think he could keep functioning if he couldn't have Maggie in his life. "Please," he said.

"I can't, Nathan," she said. "I can't keep doing this, it hurts too much."

Nathan dropped his hand from her face, the tears welling in her eyes making him feel like the biggest bastard on the planet.

"I love you," he said, pleading. "Please talk to me about this. I know we can make it work."

"I know you think you do," Maggie said, "but it's not enough. I don't trust you. I don't think I will ever be able to trust you."

Nathan broke from her now steady gaze, unable to bear what she was saying.

"I know you're trying to be honest with me about why you rejected me —"

"I wasn't rejecting," he interrupted, but before he could finish his defence, she interrupted him in turn.

"You were. You have it in your head you were doing something noble, but if you loved me the way I loved you, you couldn't have walked away from me. I barely survived losing you then. I won't survive it again."

"You wouldn't have to. I was a fool, but I know exactly how empty my life is without you. I won't make that mistake again."

"It doesn't matter what you say, Nathan. I know everybody leaves in the end; you taught me that. I don't trust you. I can't let myself trust you."

"Can you honestly tell me you don't feel anything for me?"

"It doesn't matter what I feel for you. I'd have to trust you for that to matter."

Watching Nathan over the rim of her mug, Grace sighed.

He knew she was trying to get him to open up to her, but he couldn't stop himself from asking, "Are you okay?"

"I'm fine," she said. "It's you I'm worried about."

Nathan didn't answer that; instead, he just let the silence continue. It wasn't as though she could fix anything. Maggie had made it very clear she wasn't about to give him a second chance. He wished he could blame Maggie; maybe it would hurt less if he didn't have to face the fact it was his own fault. Add in the fact that there was no telling what Rupert had said to her, and he was almost beside himself. She could be packing to go back to London, to Rupert, right now.

"You love her," Grace finally said.

"Does it matter?" Nathan asked.

"Of course it matters," she said, her hand sliding across the table and resting on his. Gone was the smooth texture of the hands that had cleaned his grazed knees and picked him up every time he'd fallen. Now her hands looked dry, not the thin crepe of real old age, but the signs that the years were passing could be read in the faint age spots that were becoming more visible on the back of her hand. Nathan knew he was just trying to distract himself. He didn't want to fall apart, but he didn't think he could keep it together in the face of his mum's compassion.

"Why did you tell me I should let her go?" he asked. By the expression on Grace's face, he knew he didn't have to elaborate. She knew exactly what he was referring to.

"I've asked myself that a lot over the years," Grace said, pulling her hand back and slipping it onto her own lap.

"I loved her. I still love her."

"I know, my darling, but you were both so young. I was afraid that one day one of you would resent the other for clipping each other's wings. You know we all see Maggie and Sarah as part of our family, and I was afraid my family was going to be ripped apart if you gave in to the attraction you obviously felt for her."

Nathan laughed at that, the sound a harsh and bitter one that he hadn't ever expected to hear reverberate around the kitchen of his parents' home. "That worked out well, didn't it?" he said.

"Don't mock me, Nathan Parker. I'm still your mother."

He knew he should apologise, but he didn't have it in him. He'd spent the last few days looking after Maggie, and while things between them were better, he didn't know if they would ever get to a place where she would forgive him. The fact that bloody Rupert had shown up didn't help either.

"Well, your little bit of advice came too late. We'd slept together the night before you decided to dish that out. You can imagine how well it went down when I had to tell her we couldn't be together after that." Nathan had expected at least a sliver of satisfaction at seeing his mother's face fall, at seeing her usually pink cheeks pale. Instead, he just felt even more crap. Apparently he had a knack for hurting the women he loved.

"Oh, Nathan," she said. "Why didn't you tell me?"

"You'd spent an hour talking to me about how much I was going to hurt Maggie if I pursued our feelings for each other. How could I admit to you that it was too late? I just went into damage control mode."

Grace stood and, taking both their mugs, tipped out the remaining tea, before putting the kettle on to make fresh cups. Nathan's had been fine, but he knew his mum well enough to know it was her way of finding some time to gather herself. Sitting silently, he fought the urge to run. Running was what had caused this mess. He had to believe there was a way to fix it.

Finally, Grace put a mug of fresh tea in front of him and sat down. "I'm truly sorry, Nathan. If I had known, I would have handled things differently."

"But you'd still have wanted to *handle* things," he said, not quite able to believe that she was standing by her interference.

"Nathan, that girl loves you as much as you love her. You will be able to work through this together."

"So that's it? No apology for the years we have lost? No concern that I won't be able to win her round?"

"You will win her round."

"I don't think so. I've explained until I was blue in the face that I loved her even then, that I was just following your advice not to tie her here, and do you know what? She doesn't care; she said in no uncertain terms she doesn't trust me to stick around, that she never will. So you tell me, how am I supposed to *fix* that?"

"To start with, you need to be honest with yourself," Grace said, taking a sip from her mug, and gone was her expression of concern. In fact, even the glimmer of guilt that had been evident since they'd started this conversation had gone.

"What? I am being honest. I love Maggie, I've told her that, I've told her what happened." Nathan loved his mum dearly, but right now he wasn't sure why he was talking about this to her.

"Nathan, if you'd been certain, if you'd been ready to be here with her forever, nothing would have stopped you, certainly not my advice."

"But you're my mum. I trust your advice."

"You don't always follow it, though," Grace said with a gentle smile. "I'm sure we could list a thousand times you've ignored it, and I've always tried to respect that, so it certainly wasn't because you felt you couldn't."

"You said I would hurt Maggie if I kept her here," Nathan said, the words coming out louder than he'd intended.

"And I know you love her, but there were other options. You could have encouraged her to finish her degree; you could have kept her focused on the options her future held and still been at her side. I admit, I was worried you wouldn't be able to, that you would be too afraid of losing her to give her that freedom, but you didn't do any of those things. You saw the option I showed you and you grabbed it."

"Thanks for sharing those other choices with me at the time," he said sharply.

"I'm not going to sit here and say I did the right thing, but hindsight is a wonderful thing. I did what I thought was best for two people I love deeply. I won't apologise for that." Grace's tone was even, but the flare in her eyes made it clear that she wasn't finding this any easier than he was.

Nathan took a sip of the still scalding tea, not really wanting it, but needing something to stop him from speaking; he couldn't let himself hurt his mum, no matter how angry he was feeling.

"Did you really end things with Maggie just for her?" Grace asked quietly.

He opened his mouth to snap back that of course he had, but a slimy feeling twisted in his stomach.

"You left here so quickly after that day."

Nathan had left so quickly because he hadn't been able to go anywhere without seeing Maggie in every object, every surface; even every building in the village was so tangled up with his memories of Maggie, that he hadn't been able to take it. He'd also been running away, making sure he wouldn't have to face her when she came back from university for Christmas. Had there been another reason, though? If he was honest, he had to admit that there had been a part of him that had wanted to travel, to see what else was out there. It had never been about anyone else, he'd never wanted to see *who* else was out there, but as Maggie had started her degree, her plan to get a good job to help support her sister and niece had been so firmly in place that he'd known he couldn't have both.

"Maybe it wasn't all about her," he said, the words feeling like a betrayal on his lips.

"Perhaps being honest with yourself is the first step to convincing Maggie you mean what you say," Grace said, her hand once again curling over his.

"Even if I could do that, her ex-boyfriend is back on the scene," Nathan said, the words snarling out as he pictured the man who'd spent the entirety of yesterday afternoon with Maggie, stealing away the last of Nathan's time before Sarah and Paul had come home.

"He's not here now, though," Grace said.

"Yes, but here or not, she's made her position clear."

Grace gave him a look of sympathy that made him simultaneously want to cry and hit something.

"How do I fix it?" Nathan asked, pleading for a solution. The fact Maggie hadn't denied having feelings for him somehow made it even worse. "If I thought there was no chance she could love me, I'd leave her alone. I'd respect that, you know I would."

Grace nodded vigorously. "I know."

"So how do I fix it? How do I make sure she chooses me?"

"I think this is something you have to work out for yourself," Grace said. "But try to remember that the lack of trust probably isn't all about you. Maggie has been through so much. She lost her parents, she feels she lost you, she's guarding her heart like it's something precious to be locked away, kept safe from the world, and she's only right about half of that."

"She said 'everyone leaves in the end'," Nathan said, remembering the words she had whispered to him in her distress. His mind swirled with the realisation that Maggie's mistrust of him was part of something so much bigger. He was such a fool, he'd been so wrapped up in how he felt that he hadn't stopped to consider everything she was dealing with.

"You need to prove to that girl that you're going to be by her side no matter who tries to turn her head, and no matter what the future holds." Agnes's voice filled the room.

Nathan looked up to see her standing in the hallway, dressed in a fluorescent pink tracksuit, a twinkle in her eye, despite the seriousness of her expression.

"I mean it, boy, you do whatever it takes to prove to her she can count on you."

"I'm trying, Gran."

"Well, obviously not hard enough if you're sitting here feeling sorry for yourself."

Nathan laughed at that; trust Gran to get straight to the heart of things.

CHAPTER TWENTY-NINE

Sipping from the plastic cup covered in miniature Santas, Maggie tried not to wince.

"It gets better by the time you're on your third glass," Susie said, tipping more of the bottle of cheap wine into her own cup.

Maggie briefly wondered whether she should be drinking less than a week after her operation, before deciding she didn't care. She was sick of being the good girl who always did what she was supposed to. She tipped her head and gulped the cup of wine before holding it out for another refill.

"I'd better get to number three quickly, then," she said, the pleasant warmth of the alcohol completely overwhelmed by the sharp taste.

"Now that's more like the Maggie I remember," Susie said, filling her cup again before discarding the empty bottle.

Leaning side by side on the low table, the women looked at the gathered group; it was the accounting firm's annual Christmas party, although 'party' was probably too kind a description. Every year, Uncle Walter invited all the customers and a few of the neighbouring businesses to join them for nibbles and drinks at lunchtime on the last day the office was open before Christmas. Maggie raised her cup to him where he was standing chatting to the local GP, Dr Marsden. The man could talk for England, and it didn't look like Walter would be escaping any time soon.

"It's lovely to have you back here," Tess said, handing Maggie a tray piled high with goodies from her bakery.

"Thanks, Tess, it's good to be back," Maggie said, surprised by how much she meant it. "Even more so if you tell me there are red velvet cupcakes here."

Tess laughed and reached into the enormous handbag that was making her lopsided as Maggie found a space on the heaving table for the tray and placed it down.

"I thought I'd better make sure you didn't miss out," Tess said, rooting around before lifting out a small cardboard box and handing it over.

"Hang on, why don't I get a special cake?" Susie asked.

"You'll eat anything," Tess laughed, taking a cup of wine from Susie, and the three of them pretended to clink their drinks before sipping in unison.

"I'd better go and speak to Walter before I've had too much to drink. Put that somewhere safe," Tess said to Maggie, gesturing to the box. "If you're not careful, Susie will nab it."

Maggie giggled with Susie as they watched Tess make her way across the room, stopping to chat to everyone she passed.

"It'll take her until next Christmas to get to Walter at that rate," Susie said.

"So," Maggie said, turning to face Susie. "Want to tell me why you've been funny with me since I came back?" Maggie took another sip of wine. Give her a difficult client and she was golden, yet as soon as it was something personal she was totally useless at sorting things out. She didn't used to be like this; she never used to be so afraid of upsetting people. *Thank goodness for alcohol*, she thought; at least it gave her the courage to find out what was going on with her old friend. Although, just how much courage could two and a bit small glasses of cheap wine give you?

Susie shifted so she could look directly at her, her gaze appraising, as though trying to work out whether or not to say something. "Fine," she said. "You vanished."

Maggie frowned; yes, she'd left, but they'd all grown up in this small village. Leaving wasn't unusual. "Lots of people leave. Nathan left and you don't seem to have a problem with him."

"I don't mean that you physically left, you just disappeared. *Poof.*" Susie's hands jerked up with the word, wine sloshing over the side of her cup. "You were my friend. I know I'm a couple of years older than you, but you know I was stuck in that class that was almost entirely boys and you were my only real female friend. You left me. I get that you needed to move away for university, for work, but you didn't need to just cut me off."

Maggie's chest tightened, her stomach churning as a hot feeling washed over her. She'd been so wrapped up in her own issues, she hadn't considered what she was doing to anyone else. "I'm sorry," she said.

Susie shrugged, turning away from her.

Heat flowed through Maggie; she'd hurt Susie and she didn't know if she could fix it. Reaching out, she lifted Susie's free hand. "I mean it, I'm sorry for being so selfish. I can't justify doing that to you. I'd like to be your friend again, though, if you'll have me. I promise I would never be so thoughtless again."

Susie studied her again, her gaze open and assessing, and Maggie held her breath. Head spinning, the realisation crashed over her that this was how Nathan had felt when he'd asked her for another chance.

"Last chance," Susie said, her expression serious.

"It's the last one I'll need," Maggie said.

Susie smiled and wrapped her arms around Maggie. "So, ready to admit you fancy Nathan?" Susie asked, whispering the words into Maggie's ear.

Maggie jumped back, her wine spilling on the carpet as she did. "What…?"

"Come on. It was obvious you fancied him back then, and it doesn't look like that's changed," Susie said, giving her a knowing grin. "The fact you didn't bother coming home once he had left for his travels made it pretty clear he was the only attraction this place had for you."

"Uhh…" Maggie floundered.

"Don't worry, I won't tell," Susie said.

"So what are you up to when you're not in here?" Maggie asked.

Susie gave her a look that made it clear she hadn't missed Maggie's clumsy attempt to change the subject, but thankfully she allowed it. "I'm doing my degree part-time. I work here and the pub to pay the fees. I want to teach art," she said, her chin tilting, as though expecting to have to defend her choice.

"That's amazing; you'd be a great teacher," Maggie said, meaning it.

"I won't be rich," Susie said with a wry smile.

"Money isn't everything," Maggie said, knowing that for her it certainly wasn't. "Not sure Dean sees it that way."

"Why, what has Dean said?" Maggie asked with a frown. The Dean she knew wasn't particularly money-oriented. Well, he loved his bonuses, and the flash cars he always bought with them, something she'd never seen the point of when you lived in London, but he never judged other people by their income.

"Nothing, just ignore me," Susie said.

"So you're an artist. I'm really pleased you're doing something with your talent; you were always drawing when we were at school," Maggie said, deciding to move the conversation forward positively.

"Susie's shared her plans with you, then?" Walter asked, wrapping an arm around Susie's shoulder.

Maggie smiled at him; despite the deep tan he'd picked up on his trip, the dark bags under his eyes gave away just how much the twenty-two-hour flight home had taken out of him. The fact he had come at all, when he couldn't have had time to do much more than dump his suitcases and head straight to the office, was testament to how much he cared about the practice.

"Have you considered my offer?" Walter asked.

Maggie swallowed; she knew that she should just say no, like she always did. Especially now that she knew she could go back to work and walk straight into the director role. She found that she couldn't make herself turn him down, not just yet anyway. Avoiding his gaze, she looked around the office, her chest pinched as she tried to imagine not coming back after the Christmas break.

"Don't worry, you don't have to answer me today. The offer is always there, and if you can't afford to buy back in, you could be the senior employee," Walter said, reaching out to touch her arm. "I'd just love to have you here, we all would."

Susie gave a nod of agreement, and Maggie swallowed, blinking back the moisture that was building in her eyes. Buying back in wouldn't be a problem, not now she knew about the bank account Sarah had secretly been paying into. Maggie hadn't realised how much she'd missed having these wonderful people in her life, and the fact that she and Susie had cleared the air made it even harder to say no.

"I'd better head home," Walter said, smiling softly at her. "Are you ladies okay to lock the office up when this lot have finished?"

Feeling a little more fuzzy-headed than she'd like at three in the afternoon, Maggie sat on the floor, her legs crossed, as she tried to untangle a ball of fairy lights while Sarah draped the first set artistically around the tree that had arrived that morning.

"We really need to get this finished before Paul gets back with Evie," Sarah said with a glance at the clock on the mantelpiece.

"I'm trying. I have no idea how anyone could tangle lights as much as this, though," Maggie said, leaning back against the couch and closing her eyes. By the time the office had emptied, she'd had at least four glasses of wine. It had been fun at the time but an hour later, not so much.

"And that's part of why we have to get this bit done before she's here: Evie's the one who put the lights in the boxes after last Christmas. I'm hoping we can get it done so when she's back we can relax and let her hang all the ornaments," Sarah said.

Leaning forward, Maggie forced herself to refocus her efforts. Decorating the tree was one of her favourite things about Christmas — well, once the boring bits were done anyway.

The sound of the front door bashing open was swiftly followed by Evie's voice.

"We got loads of presents, Mum."

"Oh well, we tried," Sarah said, rolling her eyes at Maggie with a smile.

As she skidded to a stop in the doorway, Evie's face lit up. "We're decorating the tree?"

"Yes, but not for another ten minutes, so why don't you go and get a snack?" Sarah said.

"Sorry, I thought you'd be done by now," Paul said as he entered the lounge, planting a kiss on his new wife's lips.

"Gross," Evie said as she came back into the room, arms wrapped around the biscuit barrel.

"Yes, yes, having parents who love each other is awful, I know," Paul said with a laugh.

Maggie handed Sarah the unravelled lights and she immediately began putting them on the tree.

"Evie, you don't need the whole barrel," Paul said, glancing at his daughter. "You already had a cake and hot chocolate at the café."

"I know, Dad, but Auntie Maggie might want some too," Evie said, with a grin that made it clear that thought had been secondary to unfettered access to the biscuits. "So, can we start decorating the tree now?" she added.

"Almost, go and grab the chocolates from the pantry and we'll be ready to start," Sarah said.

Standing up, Maggie grabbed her brother-in-law and pulled him in for a quick hug. "Thank you for making Sarah so happy."

"No need to thank me. I know how lucky I am," Paul said, his voice thick as he hugged her back.

The sitting room already looked like Santa's grotto. Every surface was covered in glittering ornaments, bunting hung across the ceiling. The scent of sweet pine from the large tree sitting in the bay window filled the room. Multi-coloured lights now twinkled at them, but the tree was otherwise bare.

Every year Maggie and Sarah, and later Paul, and then Evie, had decorated the room, making it as Christmassy as possible. No surface would be left untouched. It was clear they had carried on the tradition in Maggie's absence.

"Let's get started," Maggie said, with a grin at her niece as she reappeared, laden with packets of chocolates to be strung onto the tree.

"Before we do, would now be a good time?" Paul asked, looking hopefully at his wife.

"Yes, I suppose it would," Sarah said, her hand drifting to her belly.

Maggie felt her jaw drop as the implication of her sister's action sank in.

"We wanted you two to be the first to know: we're having a baby," Sarah said, her gaze focused completely on Evie, as though unsure of how her daughter would react.

"Oh my God, I'm going to have a baby sister or brother?" Evie asked, her voice a squeal of pure delight that left no doubt as to how she felt about the news.

Sarah nodded and Maggie wrapped her arms around her sister.

"I'm so happy for you," she said, her eyes filling at the thought of their little family growing. Sarah hugged her back and they made room as Evie wriggled between them. "I'm so happy for you both," Maggie added, releasing her sister and niece and hugging Paul as well. "When are you due?"

"Not until the end of May," Sarah said.

"Can we go for a girl?" Evie asked, when they all finally stopped hugging each other.

"I don't think we can choose," Paul said, mussing Evie's hair.

"I guess not," she replied, "but it would be nice to have some more girls in the family."

"I'm sure you'll love your little sibling, whether it's a boy or a girl," Maggie said with a smile.

"I will," Evie said, dancing around the room. "I'm going to be a big sister."

Maggie helped herself to a biscuit.

"Can we do the tree now?" Evie asked.

"Of course," Sarah said, clearly relieved her daughter was happy she wasn't going to be an only child anymore.

They each lifted baubles and homemade ornaments from the box, and Maggie couldn't help but compare them to the pristine, ornate decorations Rupert had in his penthouse. She wasn't really sure why he'd bothered spending so much to have professional decorators come in. When she'd suggested they do it together, he'd frowned and announced that he wasn't doing that when he wasn't bothered about Christmas. If it hadn't been for the fact he'd been schmoozing the directors of their accountancy firm by having them all round for dinner, she figured he wouldn't have bothered at all.

Somehow, despite the fact she'd done all the work for that meal, it had been Rupert it had paid off for. Maggie rolled her neck and shrugged off the bitter thought. She didn't resent his promotion, just what had come after.

Pulling the last of the ornaments out of the box, she stopped in her tracks. Frozen in place for a beat, it took her a moment to breathe past the memories that flooded her. She lifted the small angel. Its face was even grubbier than she remembered. Gently fingering the fragile silvery lace that was wrapped around the pink cardboard cone of its body, she blinked hard.

"I know I should replace it, but I haven't been able to bring myself to do it yet," Sarah said.

"Mum, you can't replace the angel. She's too special," Evie said seriously.

Maggie found herself nodding in agreement. The angel was too special to replace. Although, it did look like it could do with some TLC if it was going to last for many more years.

"Why don't you put it on, Maggie?" Sarah suggested.

Maggie looked from the angel cradled in her hands to the tree. Year after year she had placed this angel on the tree, initially being lifted by her dad, and then later balancing on her tiptoes. The scratchy heat behind her eyes intensified.

"I think Evie should do it," she said, when she finally found her voice again.

"Thanks, Auntie Maggie," Evie said, gingerly taking the angel from her outstretched hands.

Maggie sank into the armchair as Paul lifted Evie up so she could reach the top. The sight of him holding his daughter, the way her own dad had held her, warmed her and she smiled at her sister. They would always feel the loss of their own parents, but their family was growing again, and that could only be a good thing.

"Let's have some mulled wine," Sarah said. "I have some non-alcoholic stuff for me."

"Do I have to?" Maggie asked; it didn't exactly taste great, and she already had a fuzzy head from the wine earlier.

"Yes, it's Christmas," Sarah said with a smile. "Besides, Paul's off out for his skittles night. We need a girls' night in."

Paul had left hours before and now Evie was tucked into bed, Maggie had convinced Sarah to ditch the mulled wine for something that tasted good enough that people would drink it all year round.

"So, ready to tell me why you left?" Sarah asked, her expression serious as she met Maggie's surprised gaze.

Maggie swallowed hard, knowing that even if she hadn't promised Sarah she would share, she needed to talk to her sister about everything.

"It's hard to take time off from my job," Maggie said. She was going to need to build up to the really hard stuff.

"Really?" Sarah asked, her brow raised.

"Well, usually, although it might be easier now, given that they've made me redundant."

"What? Why? You're so good at your job."

"Don't worry, Rupert came here yesterday to let me know that they want me back, so I just need to decide whether to go back or join another firm."

"Rupert, is he the guy you've been seeing?"

"Yes, he wants me back too. Apparently now I've been offered the director position, he thinks he made a mistake dumping me," Maggie said, giving her sister a wry smile.

"Oh, I have questions, so many questions," Sarah said, topping up Maggie's wine glass and her own soft drink. "But firstly, director, you've wanted that for so long — why aren't you jumping for joy?"

"I don't know. You're right, I've wanted it since the day I left university, so why aren't I jumping at it? My salary would take a massive leap if I accept."

"Please don't start with that nonsense about sending money to us again. We don't need your money. We just need you," Sarah said, her expression serious.

"Uncle Walter offered me Mum's place in the practice," Maggie said, wondering what had possessed her to share that, as her sister's eyes lit up with hope.

"Well, you know we'd love to have you here full-time, and I can't say the idea of you taking over where Mum left off doesn't appeal, but you know you have my support whatever you choose. I just want you to be happy."

Maggie threw her arms around Sarah's shoulders and pulled her close. Blinking hard, she pushed her tears back. If only she knew what choice would make her happy.

"Okay," Sarah said, pulling back so she could look her directly in the face. "That still doesn't answer my original question, because you didn't have this job when you stopped coming home."

Maggie nodded, her throat closing on the words as she took a large gulp of wine before speaking. "Do you remember when I came back for the October holidays when I first started university?"

"Yes, how could I forget? My little sister went away and came back six weeks later a glamorous woman," Sarah said with a smile. "You changed so much so fast."

"Well, I wasn't as grown up as I thought I was. I threw myself at Nathan and he rejected me." Maggie studied her glass, tracing the contrasting swirl of gold that wound around the stem.

"He what?" Sarah spluttered. "But that boy was crazy about you."

Maggie's head swung up; her sister was surprised that Nathan had rejected her? "You knew I fancied him?" she asked, stunned that Sarah could have realised.

"I think it was a little more than that; you were in love with him."

"You never said anything."

"I didn't want to make you feel awkward. First love is tricky; I didn't want you to be embarrassed. I thought it was sweet, the way the pair of you circled around each other, neither of you quite brave enough to admit it."

"Well, I admitted it, I kissed him, told him I loved him, slept with him. I honestly thought that was it. That I'd get to spend the rest of my life with him. It took him less than twelve hours to change his mind and ditch me."

"That's why you stopped coming home?"

"It was too hard. Everything here reminded me of him." Maggie forced herself to look at her sister. "I'm sorry."

"I'm sorry too," Sarah said. "I can't imagine how hard it would be to be here if Paul and I broke up."

"Well, Paul's the exception."

Sarah wrapped her arms around Maggie and pulled her in for another hug. "If it's any consolation, Nathan's a moron," Sarah said, making her laugh. "I still can't understand why he'd do that, though. I was sure he was in love with you too."

"Well, you were wrong," Maggie said firmly.

"So how has it been since you've been back?"

Maggie looked at Sarah, her cheeks heating with the memory of their night in the barn.

"You didn't?" Sarah asked, her voice amused. "When?"

"While you were away. It was the night before my surgery."

"I still haven't forgiven you for doing that while I was away, and without telling me. I wanted to be with you so I could help," Sarah said. "But never mind that now. I need details."

"It was amazing," Maggie said, her mind drifting to the feel of his body against hers, to the reverent way he had touched her, as though she was something precious.

"On second thoughts, I definitely don't need details; you're still my little sister," Sarah said with a laugh. "Your expression says it all. So what now?"

"He wants to get back together. He told me he loves me."

Sarah spat her mouthful of drink out. "He loves you? Why on earth are you sitting here with me, then?"

"It's not that simple," Maggie said with a frown.

"Why not? It's obvious you love him." Sarah studied her for a long time, before asking, "Did you ever stop loving him?"

"No, I don't think I did," Maggie said, the admission somehow making her feel lighter. She didn't really understand why; it wasn't as though sharing her feelings with Sarah actually made any difference to the situation.

"So what's the problem?"

Maggie swallowed hard; could she really give voice to her fears? "I don't think I could survive losing him when he leaves again," she said, the words almost a whisper. She wished she could blame the wine for making her honest, but she knew it wasn't that. Everything had built up to the stage that it had to spill out.

She could feel Sarah studying her as she steadfastly refused to meet her sister's gaze. "Does it hurt now?" Sarah asked.

Maggie couldn't form the words; she simply nodded without looking at her sister.

"So why?"

Maggie looked up at Sarah at that. "Everybody leaves," she said flatly, knowing there was no way her sister could argue with something that held so much truth.

Sarah moved closer to her on the couch, her hand resting on Maggie's arm. "They do," she said. "I'm not going to sit here and try to make you believe otherwise, because it's true."

Maggie felt her jaw drop and realised just how much she'd been hoping her sister would try to persuade her it wasn't true. Her throat tightened as she faced the fact that there was no happy ending here.

"So how could you marry Paul if you know he's going to leave you one day? Is that why it took you so long to say yes?" Maggie asked, not sure why she was pushing it.

"No, I was terrified I was settling for him, that I was missing some big adventure out there, but I finally realised that it doesn't matter what's out there." Sarah lifted her hand to her still flat stomach and smiled. "My life with Paul is exactly the adventure I want. He might leave me one day, I might leave him, and even if we stay together, one of us will be left behind eventually because the chances of us both dying together are pretty low, despite it happening to Mum and Dad. There aren't any guarantees in life. But, Maggie, it's everything in between that matters. I know how hard it was for you when Mum and Dad died…"

Maggie opened her mouth to interrupt, to explain that she knew it had been harder for Sarah, but Sarah raised her hand to silence her, before continuing.

"Everyone leaves one day, whether that's by choice or the fact that death is unavoidable for us all at some stage. That doesn't mean that we can spend our lives avoiding connections. You shouldn't sacrifice the joy of love and relationships, whether that's family, romance or friends, just to save yourself the possibility of pain one day in the future. The pain is the price we pay for love."

"I don't know if I can," Maggie admitted.

"You're already hurting. Is holding Nathan at arm's length really going to protect your heart?" Sarah asked, and Maggie knew she didn't need to answer the question. They both knew it wasn't. "Maggie, you are strong and capable, and I think you know in your heart that the price for experiencing love is one that's worth paying."

"It's too late. I said some awful, unforgivable things to him," Maggie said.

"Well, that may be the case, but you don't know if you don't try. You have to at least try and build the life that will fill your heart with joy."

CHAPTER THIRTY

Pushing the tall glass door open, Maggie took a deep breath before walking through it.

"Miss Green, how wonderful to see you," a voice greeted her.

She smiled at James, who had been working on reception for the last couple of years, his uniform as immaculate as always. "Hi, James, how are you?" she asked.

"I'm great, Louisa and I are moving in together in the New Year," James said with a grin.

"I'm so pleased you found somewhere that works for you both," Maggie said, her smile growing. It was nice to know that at least someone had sorted their life out in the last few weeks. She hadn't managed that yet, but she was hoping today would be the first step.

"It's tiny, but it's halfway between here and her school so we can both commute easily enough. You look amazing," James said.

Maggie looked down at her jeans and boots. She'd never worn anything this casual in all the time she'd worked here, but she'd decided it was about time she stopped trying to keep her life in two separate halves. She wasn't completely sure what she wanted to do yet, but she knew that whatever choice she made, she'd do it as herself, not as the woman she thought other people wanted.

"Thank you," she smiled, not sure Henry, her boss, would agree but realising, for the first time in a long time, it wasn't the end of the world if he didn't.

"I guess you'd better head up and see the boss; he's expecting you," James said, holding out a plastic access card to her.

"Thanks, James," Maggie said, taking it from him. It was strange not to be using her own card, but she hadn't bothered going to her apartment to collect it. To be fair, she wouldn't expect it to still be active, even if she had.

Reaching the top of the building, she took a couple of steps towards Henry's office, resolutely determined to ignore the eyes that followed her.

"Maggie," cried out a voice, and she turned to see Jess, her work friend, moving towards her.

"Jess, I'm sorry I haven't answered your calls," Maggie said as Jess caught up with her. Jess was the person she really had been sorry to have been avoiding.

"Don't worry. I need to talk to you, though." Jess's expression was serious as her head moved around, as though trying to decide where to go so they would have some privacy.

"Miss Green," Henry called, his head gesturing for her to join him in his office.

Maggie shook Jess's arm from hers. "I'd better go," she said with a small smile.

Jess looked from Henry's retreating back to Maggie again, taking a deep breath, as though not sure whether to insist on speaking to her first, before shrugging. "Okay, but do not leave without speaking to me."

Maggie nodded her agreement and headed towards her old boss's office. Standing in the doorway, she felt an apprehension that she hadn't felt for a very long time in Henry's presence. She'd been through so much in the last few weeks that it felt as though the world should have changed in some dramatic way, yet standing here, she realised nothing was different. The dark wooden furniture still dominated the space; the floor-to-ceiling window still gave a view of the city that was nothing short of spectacular. The sight of the festive lights twinkling like a blanket, covering everything in sight, was the same as it was every Christmas.

"Take a seat, Maggie," Henry said.

Maggie slipped into a chair opposite his desk without thinking.

"I have to say, I was extremely disappointed with your actions," he said.

"I'm sorry?" Maggie said, shocked at his tone. She'd come here expecting an apology, and a request for her to return, not to be reprimanded.

"We have worked together for many years, and I'd like to think I've always supported you and your career," Henry said.

"And you did," Maggie replied with a frown.

"So you can imagine my disappointment that, not only did you resign without speaking to me, but that even when we offered you the promotion you have always told me you wanted, you didn't jump at the chance to return."

Resign? What the hell was he talking about?

"Are you seriously going to sit here and try to make this my fault?" Maggie asked, her words coming out louder than she had intended.

"I don't think getting emotional is necessary," Henry replied calmly, studying her, as though not sure what to do with this version of her. She was a version so unlike the cool calm and poised woman he was used to dealing with.

"I have to admit to being a little emotional, but I think it's justified. I get a letter advising me I've been made redundant the day my extended leave is due to begin, and you're acting as though I somehow let you down."

"Redundant? What do you mean redundant? You resigned and didn't even give us any notice. I appreciate that you had an extended period of leave booked, but you know full well that a robust handover would have been necessary for someone of your seniority."

"I didn't resign, you made me redundant." Maggie reached for her handbag and pulled out the letter that was battered from being carried around since the day she received it. Placing it on Henry's desk, she sat back and crossed her arms, waiting for him to read it.

"I don't understand," he said. "I didn't approve this. I'd just confirmed your promotion to director with HR. You were going to get the news once you were back from your break. I still want you to be our new director; that's why I asked Rupert to track you down." He looked up at her, the confusion in his face deep and honest.

Sinking further into her chair, Maggie tried to make sense of things. Who would have asked Rupert to give her the letter if it wasn't from Henry? "Rupert," she said, the name slipping out as her brain spun through the implications of Henry's revelation.

"Rupert gave you this letter?"

Maggie nodded.

Henry turned away, his expression darkening as he looked out sightlessly over the city. "I knew he was ambitious, but if he did this, he's ruthless."

Maggie didn't speak. The betrayal squeezed at her heart. No wonder he'd broken up with her. There was no way he could have risked her running into anyone in the firm and finding out the truth.

"Could you wait here? I'll just be a few minutes," Henry asked, studying her carefully.

When she nodded, he slipped out of his office, leaving her in the silence that his reinforced glass office walls created.

Unable to sit still, Maggie walked over to the window, placing her palm on the cold glass as she studied the view. The city sprawled ahead of her, the view she had coveted for more years than she wanted to admit to. She knew she could still have it, and without the pain of being dropped by the firm — maybe she did want it? After all, it was only thinking that they hadn't wanted her, hadn't valued her, that had made her start to reconsider her future. If this hadn't happened, if Rupert hadn't happened, nothing would have changed.

His name registering in her thoughts sent the sense of betrayal through her again, but already, it wasn't as sharp as it had been just moments ago. Maggie couldn't pretend she didn't already know that Rupert was prepared to do whatever it took to succeed. His determination and drive had been one of the things that had initially attracted her to him. It was the fact he was prepared to treat her that way as well that she was struggling with. Had he even wanted to get back together? Or had it all been part of covering his back now he'd been instructed to get her back on board at the firm? Why had he been so determined she would say yes? Surely if he wanted to cover his tracks, the best outcome would have been her saying no. He would have earned brownie points for trying and his secret would have remained hidden.

Did any of it really matter? Maggie's eyes glazed over as she pictured her life over the last few weeks. Gone were the sleek suits and meetings where the stakes were millions of pounds. Gone were the evenings spent in wine bars, or poring over documents. In their place had been jeans, her mother's shabby desk and clients whose finances ran into the hundreds or thousands, rather than millions, and evenings with her family, with Nathan.

Sucking in a deep breath, Maggie stepped back from the window and sat back down, her arms resting comfortably on her lap.

When Henry reappeared, he gave her a determined look. "Right, we have a plan to fix all of this," he said. "Firstly, I want you to know that as soon as we became aware of your departure, we attempted to contact you and remedy the situation. Unfortunately, you were not answering your mobile and we had no other way of contacting you. As far as we are concerned, nothing has changed. Your role remains yours and we will sort out the salary you should have been paid over the last few weeks."

"So, I'm not redundant?"

"Maggie, you are our best account manager, we would not wish to lose you, and if you want it, the directorship is yours."

"So you what, are offering me the directorship to apologise for the mistake?" Maggie wasn't really sure why she was asking, but she knew she had to completely understand what was on offer and why.

"No, you would have received that in the New Year anyway. We will just make it official now."

Maggie smiled; she'd wanted it for so long that to actually be here, in Henry's office, being told she had done it was an incredible feeling.

"You'll be the youngest director in our history; you just need to say yes," Henry said, smiling at her, the curl of his lip making it clear he was certain of her answer.

"And Rupert?"

"There will be a full investigation; obviously I don't anticipate him remaining with this division."

Maggie knew that even while Henry was going to be annoyed at Rupert, there would be part of him that would admire the steps he'd taken to get what he wanted. There was no way the firm would want to let him go completely. That degree of ruthlessness was what had made the company what it was today.

She turned, looking out at the floor of desks surrounded by external facing offices for the directors. She'd be allocated one of those offices. She'd get to spend her days leading the incredible team of people out there, and helping the business to continue growing and thriving. Her heart stuttered; she should be overwhelmingly delighted, yet she realised that this wasn't her dream anymore.

Turning back to Henry, Maggie gave him a small smile. "Thank you, Henry," she said. "Thank you for everything you have done for me, thank you for this incredible offer, but —"

"Don't," Henry said. "Don't turn it down just yet. You'll regret it if you do. At least take some time to think about it."

"I have thought about it," Maggie explained. "I know this isn't the answer you want, but I am saying no. I can't tell you how much your mentorship has meant to me, or how much this offer means to me, but this isn't what I want anymore."

"What do you want, then?" Henry asked with a frown.

Maggie resisted the urge to laugh at his confusion; he was a corporate man through and through, and she knew he would struggle to understand why anyone wouldn't want this life. "I'm not planning to stay in London. I'm going to go and run my mum's old accountancy firm."

"Oh," Henry said, leaning back into his chair. "So you won't be going to a competitor?"

And there it was, the real heart of the matter. Maggie didn't doubt that Henry meant well, that he cared about her — well, as much as he cared about anyone who worked for him — but at the end of the day, it was the company that held his heart.

"No, I promise you I wouldn't do anything to hurt the company." Standing up, Maggie shook his hand. "Thank you," she said. "Oh, and about Rupert."

"What about him?"

"You don't need to lose both of us, not on my account anyway."

Henry blinked at her, surprise etched in his face. "Thank you, Maggie, for everything."

Stepping out of his office, Maggie decided she'd track Rupert down before she caught up with Jess; at least that way she could relax and enjoy her friend's company. She hadn't told him she was coming today, and she now understood why he hadn't wanted her to come in until everything was resolved.

"Maggie," Jess called to her. "Can we catch up?"

"I was just going to see Rupert. Could we catch up afterwards?"

"I really need to speak to you before you see him," Jess said, her corkscrew curls bouncing as she headed over to Maggie and grabbed her arm, before leading her into a meeting room.

Maggie frowned slightly at her friend's concerned expression. "What's wrong?"

"Look, I'm really sorry to have to tell you this but you need to know."

Jess's tone, so at odds with her usual happy demeanour, made Maggie pause. "Okay," she said, following Jess's lead and slipping into one of the chairs that surrounded the massive meeting table.

"Did Henry tell you about the promotion?"

"Yes," Maggie said slowly, surprised it would be public knowledge.

"Did you know he'd offered Rupert a directorship as well, but only if he could get you to come back?" Jess said, her words coming out harshly.

Maggie sank back into the chair. There it was, the final piece of the puzzle. The real reason he'd been so determined to get her back. "Thank you so much for telling me, Jess. I can't tell you how much it means to me that you would look out for me like this, and I'm sorry I didn't answer your calls."

"That's not all," Jess said darkly. "I can't promise its true, but the rumour mill is saying that on the last day before your holiday, Rupert was caught screwing one of the trainees in the boardroom."

Maggie considered the allegation; office gossip wasn't always right, but she'd worked here for long enough to know that, more often than not, it was close enough. Even if this rumour wasn't true, the fact that it was so easy for her to believe told her everything she needed to know. She waited for the pain to hit. The realisation that she had given so many years to someone who was prepared to treat her this way should hurt, it should be a gut-wrenching agony, but it wasn't.

Maggie smiled at Jess. "Thank you," she said, leaning forward to give her friend a hug.

"Don't you believe me?" Jess asked, her concern slipping into something harder.

"Yes, I do," Maggie said, "and I guess I should be more upset, but I just don't care." She didn't realise how true her words were, how certain she was in her decision, until she'd said the words out loud. Going home had made her face up to how uncomfortable she'd become in her own skin, and perhaps now she was finally starting to feel like herself again, to appreciate her own value.

"Good for you," Jess said, clearly relieved to be believed, as well as outraged on her behalf. "He doesn't deserve your energy."

"He really doesn't," Maggie said with a smile, knowing that she was going to go and see him anyway. Maybe she wasn't as completely comfortable with herself as she wanted to think, yet.

Watching Rupert from the back of his cubby, Maggie folded her arms over her chest. He was leaning back in his chair, one arm behind his head as the other held the phone he was almost shouting into. She hadn't realised before just how much of his behaviour was about trying to prove himself to other people. Winking at the now pale-faced new trainee who sat in the cubby next to Rupert, Maggie wondered briefly whether this was the girl he'd been caught shagging. The thought lingered just long enough for her to feel a brief flash of pity that the girl had been sucked in by his superficial charm, just like she had been.

As Rupert finished his call, he replaced the phone handset and turned his chair slightly, as though waiting for the inevitable praise from the trainee for his masterful handling of the client he'd been speaking to. The moment he spotted Maggie standing behind him was almost a comedic masterclass. The swift double take, the dropped jaw, the spluttered attempts to string a sentence together were too perfect.

Maggie raised her eyebrows and let him flail. She'd made her choice, but that didn't mean she was about to make this moment comfortable for him.

"Um, I didn't realise you were coming in? I thought we agreed you'd call me first," Rupert said.

"I thought you'd be pleased to see me," Maggie said with a shrug.

"Oh, yes, well, of course I'm pleased to see you," he said, his smile not quite reaching his eyes. As he made a move to step towards her, hands lifting as though he would draw her into his arms, Maggie raised her eyebrows again.

"I don't think so, do you?" she said, with a pointed look at his arms, which dropped back down with pleasing swiftness.

Registering the sudden lack of noise surrounding them, Rupert's gaze swung from side to side. "We should speak in private," he said, taking in the dozens of eyes turned their way.

"I'm good here," Maggie said with a smile.

"But, Maggie, I don't want to make you feel uncomfortable," Rupert said, leaning closer and lowering his voice. "I know you don't like it when people bring their personal relationships into work; we should go somewhere private."

Maggie just stared at him for a beat. Was he really trying to make out that he was worried about her? "What personal relationship?"

"Well, you're here, surely that means we can forget all the silliness of the last few weeks and get back to normal."

"Silliness, you mean like when you falsified company documents to make me believe I'd been made redundant?" Maggie said, and the part of her that she had been trying to ignore for all these years cheered at the sight of his wide eyes.

"I don't know what you're talking about. Surely you know the firm are just trying to cover up the fact they made a mistake so they can get you back?" Rupert said.

A small part of her admired that he was still trying, but it was a very small part. "Really? So you hadn't found out that I was being given the directorship and decided to get me out of the way so you could swoop in and steal it?"

The girl next to them gasped, and Maggie gave her a wry look.

"You're just sour because I dumped you," Rupert said, all efforts to be conciliatory gone; in their place was the snarl she'd been expecting from the start of the conversation.

"Well, dumping me the day you lied about me being out of a job wasn't exactly classy, but thank you for that. You've made me realise what I really want."

"Listen, darling, if you think I'll beg for you to take me back I won't, so you should just admit you want me. You want your directorship, so we can just pretend none of this happened."

"So, that's your pitch? You think if you can convince me we should be together you'll get to keep the offer to be a director as well?" At his shocked look, Maggie smiled, a big, genuine smile. "You seriously thought I wouldn't find out that the firm offered to make you a director as well, but only if you could persuade me to come back? At least I know why you came crawling to me, pleading for me to take you back."

"Rupert, you said you loved me," the girl said, her tone thin, pain clear in every word.

"I'm so sorry, but you deserve a hell of a lot better than someone as self-centred as Rupert. Finding someone with a moral compass would be a good place to start." Maggie was vaguely aware she should be annoyed at this young woman. After all, she wasn't entirely blameless; it had been common knowledge she and Rupert were a couple, but at the end of the day, it was Rupert who had betrayed her, not some girl she didn't even know.

"So, are you taking the job?" Rupert asked.

"No, I'm not. It's a great opportunity, but it's not what I want anymore. At least you helped me to see that, so you haven't been a complete waste of my time."

"What do you mean you're not taking the job? You have to," he said, his face starting to go red.

"I don't have to do anything, Rupert, and it's not like you care; your only interest is in how it affects you."

"I bet you just loved dragging me into the dirt with Henry, didn't you? I can just picture you, acting like the perfect spoilt princess. You don't deserve that job, you weren't even prepared to fight for it. You just rolled over and left. Look at you now; I don't even know you anymore. You're wearing jeans for Christ's sake."

The look of disgust on Rupert's face as he gestured to Maggie's outfit made her look down, checking there wasn't some weird stain on her outfit. No, everything was exactly as it had been when she'd boarded the train that morning. He was genuinely that appalled to see her in an outfit that was a staple of pretty much every normal adult's wardrobe.

Maggie shrugged. "I like them."

"Great, you're happily losing all sense of style. In fact, you're just losing all sense and I lose out on a promotion, damn it."

"You might lose more than that," Maggie said, "given what you've done."

Rupert's face blanched as the meaning of her words sank in. He leaned closer to her, the malice in his face making her question her decision to speak to him at all. In that moment, she believed he could actually hit her. "You bitch, I bet you enjoyed stirring things enough for that. You want me to lose everything."

"I didn't do anything, Rupert," Maggie said, fighting to keep her tone calm as she took a step back from him. "If you get fired it will be because of your actions, not mine."

Without waiting for him to reply, she lifted the small box he'd left with her from her pocket and placed it on his desk before turning away. Ignoring the myriad sympathetic and stunned faces watching her, Maggie started towards the hallway that would take her to the lifts and back out of the building.

"This is about him, isn't it?" Rupert called after her. When she didn't reply, he shouted again, "This is about that bastard that was in your house when I came to see you. Men don't walk around barefoot unless they've been made to feel *very* welcome."

Maggie smiled at the thought of a barefoot Nathan, but smoothed her face before she turned to face Rupert one last time. "No, Rupert, it's not about him. This is about me. For the first time in forever, this is all about me."

CHAPTER THIRTY-ONE

"Wake up, wake up, wake up," chanted a high-pitched voice in Maggie's ear, the bed around her moving up and down in time with the words. She prised one eye open to see Evie bouncing up and down on her hands and knees next to her. "Hooray, you're awake," Evie squealed. "It's Christmas, Auntie Maggie. Come and see if Santa has been."

Maggie fought back a groan as she looked at the clock. Seven-fifteen. After a quick call to Uncle Walter, she'd had a few glasses of wine with Jess and time had passed so quickly she'd ended up running for the last train home, which had been followed by a night tossing and turning. She could have done with a lie in. However, one look at Evie's excited face and she couldn't deny her gorgeous niece anything.

"Has he eaten the cookies?"

"I don't know. Mum and Dad said to wait for you so we could look together."

Maggie felt her heart swell. Sarah and Paul had only been home from their honeymoon for a few days; they should have been in a bubble of romance. Instead, they were focused on making Christmas special for Evie, and for her, something they had been doing since her parents had died. Maggie might not have everything, or rather everyone, that she wanted, but she was truly blessed.

"Come on then, pumpkin. Let's go and find out." Pulling on her dressing gown over her penguin print pyjamas, she slipped her feet into her slippers and followed Evie out of her bedroom and down the hallway to where Sarah and Paul were waiting. They headed downstairs and Maggie paused at the sight of the empty hallway table. "Where are the cookies? Did Santa eat the plate too?" she teased Evie.

"No, silly, we put them in Grandma's house," Evie giggled, grabbing Maggie's hand as she dragged her along the hallway to the front door.

"We're going next door?" Maggie asked, horrified.

"Yes, the whole family is here so we wanted to do Christmas morning together," Sarah said. "Don't worry, everyone will still be in their pyjamas, and you look fine."

Maggie stared at her sister. Everyone might be in their pyjamas, but they wouldn't all have crazy bed head and be functioning on less than two hours' sleep. Was it pathetic that she didn't want Nathan to see her looking like this? It was bad enough that she was going to have to face him, to somehow find the courage to have the conversation she knew she couldn't avoid, but to do it looking like this? Without the armour of her make-up and a carefully selected outfit? No, it was too much.

"Come on, Auntie Maggie, I wanna see if Santa has been." Evie tugged on her hand.

Maggie looked down at her niece and forced a smile. What the hell, she was trying to be herself — well, this was it. She'd spent most of her childhood running in and out of the Parker family home, generally in a mud-covered princess dress, so this wasn't the worse she'd ever looked. "Okay, let's go. Do you think you've been good enough for Santa?" she asked, teasing Evie.

"I think so. I help Mum and Dad, and I always eat my broccoli, even though I hate it," Evie said as she turned, her face all wrinkled up at the thought, making Maggie giggle.

Much as it was going to hurt seeing Nathan after she had pushed him away, and as much as she was dreading having to apologise to him, dreading trying to find a way to be friends again, Maggie was grateful to be with her family. As they let themselves into the Parker house, Evie ran ahead and Maggie took the opportunity to grab her sister and pull her into a hug. "Thank you," she said, fighting back the tears.

Sarah squeezed her tight before pulling back just enough to meet her eyes. "Thank you for what?"

"For everything. There aren't words for how much I appreciate you." Maggie hugged Sarah tight again. This incredible woman had given up so much to raise her, and continued to make her a central part of her new family. Maggie was so lucky, and that was a feeling she would hang on to, even when her fears tried to remind her she'd lose even Sarah one day.

Heading into the kitchen, they found Grace pouring cups of tea from a huge pot. "Happy Christmas, help yourselves before we go through. I think we might be a while," she said, gesturing to the cups.

Maggie gave her a quick hug and, picking up a mug, walked through to the lounge.

"Santa has been, Santa has been," Evie shouted as Maggie eased herself between Dean and Joe on the couch.

"I can see that," she laughed. "I'm surprised we fit in here with all of your presents." She leant into Dean, enjoying the reassuring presence of her friend as she took in the sight of the tree. It was now surrounded by a wide mountain of gifts that seemed to spill halfway across the room.

"They aren't all for me, Auntie Maggie." Evie frowned at her.

Maggie giggled at her seriousness. "Thank goodness, you would be buried under a pile of wrapping paper if they were."

Maggie looked around the room and smiled. Chris was sitting on the floor by his wife, rubbing her feet. Arthur sat with his arm around Grace as they both sipped at mugs of tea. Sarah had sat herself next to Joe's girlfriend Kate and was poised with pen and paper. It was a habit Sarah had picked up from their mum; she had always made a list on Christmas Day of who had bought what presents, something they could never remember without the list, and they had to remember so they could write their thank-you notes. These days most people sent texts, or just called to say thanks, but Maggie and Sarah, and now Evie, still wrote the traditional thank-you letters their mum had taught them to write. Somehow, making that extra effort seemed important when people had been kind enough to buy them a gift. Although, looking at the pile that was almost certainly mostly for Evie, Maggie didn't envy her niece the task this year.

"Oh Maggie, it's beautiful," Grace said, as she lifted the chenille scarf to her face.

Maggie smiled warmly at her, pleased she had chosen her gift right. Knowing the wedding would take up all their free time, she had purchased Grace and Arthur's gifts weeks ago in London, before she'd come home.

As they all unwrapped presents around her, Maggie leant back into the couch and took a sip of her tea. The warmth of being with her extended family filled her, and she smiled at Dean when he squeezed her hand. She tried to ignore the pain that threatened to swamp her whenever her mind drifted to how her conversation with Nathan was likely to go. No matter how hard she tried, she couldn't picture the outcome she really wanted, but she knew she had to try, if for no other reason than the fact she wasn't about to step out of the lives of all the people around her again. She needed her family, and she had finally accepted that they wanted her in their lives as well. She tried to ignore the pain at the thought of having to face Nathan regularly if he wouldn't forgive her. She needed to hang on to the joy that her family would bring her.

Maggie closed her eyes, fighting the tears that welled. Drawing in a deep breath, she resolved to make the most of today. That was what she had to do, just focus on making the best of every day, appreciate every moment with these special people, these moments that would carry her through until she could see Nathan without regret. She gave herself a mental slap. She was acting as though the outcome was set in stone. She had to try; only then would she let herself admit defeat.

Maggie opened her eyes and blinked at the sight of Nathan staring at her. His eyes were tight. Great, not only was she feeling so wretched, she hadn't even managed to hide it from him. She forced a smile, for his benefit, before looking away. Evie was rustling away, surrounded by discarded paper and leaping to her feet to hug the giver every time she opened a present. It didn't seem to matter whether it was big or little, the undiluted pleasure she got from every gift was wonderful, and Maggie felt her smile shift, becoming more genuine.

When the gifts were all open, Grace lifted herself from her seat to gather up the discarded paper, only to be stopped by Paul.

"Stay there, Mum," he said. "Evie and I will clear up, won't we Evie?"

"Of course we will, Grandma," Evie said with a smile.

Everyone was relaxing and chatting about their presents when Nathan spoke up. "Um, Evie, I think you might find there is another present behind the couch." He shifted in his chair as he spoke, keeping his attention on Evie.

She grinned at her uncle and shot behind the couch before coming back out with a badly wrapped package in the palm of her hand.

"The tag says it's for you, Auntie Maggie." Evie carefully passed it to Maggie.

Maggie frowned; she had already had her gifts from Grace and Arthur, and from her sister and Paul. If she hadn't seen the surprise on Evie's face, she would have assumed it was from her; it could certainly have been wrapped by a child.

Maggie studied the oddly shaped package in her hands.

"Open it then, Auntie Maggie," Evie instructed, bouncing on her toes as she stared at the package.

Oddly nervous with everyone's eyes on her, Maggie reached for the edge of the paper with a shaky hand and pulled. The action revealed pale wood. She glanced at Nathan, who was perching on the edge of his chair, his whole body leaning towards her, his expression tense.

Removing the rest of the wrapping, she gasped; enclosed was a palm-sized high-heeled shoe. Running her fingers over the smooth surface, she turned it in her hand. The other side revealed an intricately carved inscription.

For Maggie, who deserves to feel like a princess every single day

Maggie's eyes flickered up to Nathan's. He gave her a half smile and that was the final straw. Her emotions flooded to the surface. Eyes prickling with tears, she jumped up and, ignoring the half questions and calling of her name, she ran away.

Chest heaving, Maggie reached the front door and, through the tears that were now streaming down her face, she pulled at the latch, trying to get the stupid thing undone so she could escape. She'd told him she didn't trust him, that she never would, and he'd made her a beautiful, intensely personal gift.

She couldn't be here, she had to be in control to speak to him, to explain how stupid she'd been.

"Maggie." Nathan's voice was quiet, his tone pleading.

Maggie knew he hadn't meant to upset her, knew he thought he was being kind, but she couldn't take any more. She had to pull herself together enough to talk to him properly. She needed to get away.

As she continued to fumble with the lock he caught up to her, resting his hand on her shoulder to get her attention. The heat of his palm seemed to spread through her as her body reacted to his touch. Giving up on the lock, her shoulders slumped and she sank to the floor.

"Please don't," Maggie said, not really knowing what she didn't want him to do.

"Maggie," Nathan whispered, and he placed his fingers under her chin, gently lifting her face upwards, forcing her to meet his eyes as he lowered himself to the floor next to her. "I have been a fool and I don't deserve you. You were right to say you don't trust me. You were right because I wasn't being honest. When I left back then, it wasn't just for you. I was scared. I loved you, but I was young, and stupid, and selfish. I ran and I made you feel you weren't enough. I made you feel people can't be trusted. I know I don't deserve it but, if you give me another chance, I promise to work every day to prove you can trust me. I promise to make you feel like a princess every day for the rest of our lives." His voice broke on the words, but she could hear them.

"But, I said those awful things," Maggie whispered, the words barely coherent through her tears.

"I'm not going to pretend it didn't hurt, to hear you say you didn't trust me when I was trying so hard to be honest with you, but you were right, and I needed to hear you. I love you, Maggie, I have always loved you."

"You left," she said simply. Deciding to be brave, to try to get past her fears was one thing, actually doing it was so much harder.

"I thought I was doing the right thing. I thought you needed the chance to find a life outside of the small corner of the world we lived in together. I thought I needed that as well." Nathan ran his hand through his hair, mussing it up even further.

"You broke me."

"I know I hurt you, but no one could break you. You are too strong. Just look at everything you have been through and everything you have achieved. I wish I could take it back, but I can't. Please forgive me. Please give me another chance. I'll move to London, I'll go anywhere with you. I gave you my heart a long time ago and it will always be yours."

Maggie looked at him, at the uncertainty in his eyes as he studied the penguins on her pyjamas. Nathan really didn't know what she was going to say. For once he wasn't sure of himself, was genuinely worried. He had bared his soul to her, too exposed to meet her gaze any longer. If he could make that leap of faith, then she owed it to herself to do the same.

She allowed the tiny flicker of happiness inside her to well up, and with a smile she reached up and touched his hand. "My heart has always been yours," she whispered.

His eyes snapped to hers and he stared at her for a heartbeat, as though searching for the truth in her words. Finally, when she thought he would stay silent, he pulled her close. "I love you, Maggie Green."

"I love you, Nathan Parker."

Her lips found his with a hunger she hadn't felt since they had kissed for the very first time, all those years ago. Winding her arms around him, she sank into the sensation of the man she loved holding her, his hands in her hair as they poured years of need into that moment.

Suddenly Nathan pulled back, and Maggie found herself mourning the loss of contact. He picked the wooden shoe up from where she had dropped it on the floor. "It opens," he said, handing it to her.

Maggie frowned. What? Mere seconds ago they had been kissing as if their lives depended on it, and now he was telling her about the shoe. Then it hit her. "When did you make this?" she asked, taking the beautiful carving from him.

"Yesterday and most of last night."

Maggie lifted her hand and gently smoothed the dark shadows under his eyes with her index finger. "That explains these, then."

Nathan shrugged. "I owe you more than one sleepless night."

She gave an embarrassed smile, knowing her own eyes looked a great deal worse.

"Here," he said, drawing her attention back to the shoe in her hand. He showed her the lever built into the flower carving on the toe of the shoe so the whole front tilted open.

Maggie gasped as the motion caused something glinting to fall into her palm. She looked up at Nathan.

"Maggie Green, you have been my best friend since you were born. You have been the love of my life since I was old enough to know what love is. No matter what the future holds, I promise to spend my life making you feel like the princess you deserve to be. Will you marry me?"

Maggie looked down at the man who was everything she had ever wanted and realised that she might lose him one day, but she wasn't about to throw away the chance of today and all the days between now and then. "Yes," she said, her voice cracking on the word. "Yes, absolutely yes," she repeated, wanting her answer to be clear and certain, just as she was.

Nathan slipped the ring on her finger, but she couldn't take her eyes from his face as he wrapped his arms around her and tilted her back, claiming her lips with his own. Around them, whooping and cheering echoed down the hallway. Smiling, they turned to face the doorway to the lounge and laughed at the sight of their families clapping and smiling at them.

Turning her face back to the man she had loved her whole life, Maggie pulled him back to her for another kiss. For the first time in her life she didn't want to feel like a princess, she just wanted to feel like herself.

CHAPTER THIRTY-TWO

Studying the stitching along the inside of her thigh, Maggie followed the line all the way to her ankle, where her cobalt blue stilettos reflected the strip lights fixed to the ceiling, and smiled to herself. She might have reached a stage where she was, once again, choosing jeans over just about any other type of clothing, but she didn't think she'd ever go back to trainers. Her shoes were just too fabulous.

Twitching as yet another name was called in the waiting room, she forced herself to sit still. Fidgeting wasn't going make her feel any better.

She distracted herself by shifting her hand, admiring the small pink gem that glinted every time she moved. With a round stone, set into a traditional gold band, the ring was as different from the huge diamond Rupert had given her, as the man who'd given it to her. This was a ring chosen by someone who knew her soul. She just hoped that whatever she found out today, she wasn't going to lose Nathan.

Maggie glanced up to see a tight-jawed Nathan standing in front of her, as though she'd conjured him with her thoughts.

"You can't keep doing this stuff without me," he said, a sharpness to his tone that made her want to argue, despite knowing he was right.

"I, um. I —" she began, not sure what to say.

"Don't try it," he said, sinking into the vinyl covered seat next to her, dragging his hand down his face.

Maggie folded her arms, waiting for the inevitable.

"I'm going to be your husband, you can't leave me out of things like this," Nathan said.

She felt her jaw drop. "You still, um, still want to —" she began, before tapering off.

Nathan dropped his hands and stared at her, his brow furrowed. "Maggie, I want to marry you, I'm going to marry you, no matter what, but that doesn't mean I'm not going to be mad at you sometimes. For Christ's sake, I had to find out you have an appointment with your consultant from your sister. Of course I'm going to be mad. I want to be with you, I want to be there for you, but you have to let me."

Heat rose, travelling up Maggie's chest and neck; knowing Nathan was right didn't make asking for his support easier. "I'm sorry," she said quietly. "It's hard to ask."

"I know," he whispered, pulling her closer so he could place his forehead against hers. "I understand it's going to take time for you to get used to relying on someone else, on me, but please, please don't cut me out of things that are this important."

"I'll try," she said. "It's just hard to really accept that anyone would want to be here for this. I guess I thought I could just find out and tell you after."

"Maggie, no one wants to be here for this; it's awful, waiting to find out whether or not they or someone they love is going to be okay. What you need to understand is that the thought of you doing this without me is worse. I don't care that it's awful, I want to be by your side, for everything, the good and the bad. I want to support you in every moment of your life, and I hope you want to do the same for me." Nathan lifted his hand and cradled Maggie's cheek, forcing her gaze up to meet his eyes. The sincerity in his expression took her breath away and she nodded.

"I do," she said, the thought of how hurt she would be if things were reversed and he was excluding her, making her understand, and believe, what he was saying.

"Miss Green," a voice called, and her stomach dropped.

"Yes," Maggie said, her voice breaking on the word as she stood up, preparing to follow the nurse who had called her name. Turning to her side, she slipped her hand into Nathan's and, expression tight, nodded. "I'm going to screw up. I'm going to make mistakes and shut you out sometimes, but I love you, and I want to be with you. I want this," she said, nodding to their joined hands.

"I know," Nathan said. "But so am I. I won't shut you out, but I'm going to screw up in other ways. I've actually never had a proper relationship, so I'm going to get things wrong, but we can do this. Now, let's go and find out what we're facing."

"Together," she said, squeezing his hand and walking towards the consultant's office.

CHAPTER THIRTY-THREE

Standing in front of the mirror and running a brush through her hair in an attempt to make it look less like a bird's nest, Maggie smiled at Nathan's reflection as he stood behind her, his hands snaking around her waist.

"Everyone will be here before we know it; would you give me a hand taking the food through?" he asked, a smile in his voice.

"Sure, I don't know why you wanted us to make so much, though. You know your mum is going to bring enough to last the next few weeks."

"I just want everything to be perfect," he said, nuzzling her neck.

"You're here, it's already perfect."

"I'm sorry the place isn't more finished," Nathan said, his words coming out as a sigh.

Twisting in his arms, Maggie wrapped her arms around his neck. "Nathan Parker, will you stop it. I'd live with you anywhere; a half converted barn with running water and electricity is not exactly a hardship."

"I just want everything to be…"

"Perfect, I know," she said, interrupting him with a smile. She pulled his head down to meet hers, lips joining, and she sighed with satisfaction as he sank into the kiss, all thoughts of perfection forgotten.

"Oops, sorry." Grace's voice made them jump apart. "We just let ourselves in."

"Lovely to see you both," Maggie said, accepting a hug from Arthur and a wrapped package from Grace. "What's this?" she asked, surprised to be receiving a gift when Christmas had been and gone.

"It's a housewarming gift," Grace said with a smile.

"Oh I see, I move in and get nothing. Maggie moves in with me and she gets a gift?" Nathan asked, his tone one of mock annoyance as he hugged his mum.

"It's for you both," Grace explained, rolling her eyes good-naturedly.

"Better open it, then," Nathan said, nodding at Maggie.

Maggie opened the paper of the surprisingly heavy gift. As she pulled back the shiny wrapping, her jaw dropped open. It was a perfect replica of a helter-skelter slide.

"We figured you'd never actually have a real one in here, but we wanted you to have a reminder of all the fun you always planned to have in this barn," Grace said.

Maggie's eyes filled, and she gingerly placed the ornament on the table before flinging her arms around Grace. "Thank you, thank you both so much," she said, pulling an uncomfortable-looking Arthur towards her so she could wrap an arm around him as well.

"Thanks, Mum, thanks, Dad," Nathan said.

Grace pulled back from Maggie and gently brushed her thumbs under Maggie's eyes. "Right, that's enough of that," she said. "Time to get this New Year's party going."

Maggie smiled at her, and as Nathan and Arthur went outside to bring in what was undoubtedly going to be the mountain of food Grace had prepared, she and Grace carried the plates and glasses through to Nathan's workspace, which had been tidied up for the evening. His masterpieces all hidden under a sheet on one side of the room, the remaining space had been filled with a myriad of mismatched chairs and tables that were set up to make the evening as comfortable as possible, despite the still unfinished nature of the room. Space heaters pumped out warmth, and lights were spread around the room to give a cosy feel.

"I know it would have been nicer to have the party at your house, but I really appreciate you letting us host it here," Maggie said to Grace, as they juggled plates of food, attempting to fit them on the trestle tables that had been set up along one wall.

"It's lovely to have it here," Grace said, putting her plates down. "I'm so pleased everything is working out for you and Nathan."

Over the next hour, Maggie and Nathan welcomed the various members of their family, revelling in the simple pleasure of being surrounded by the people they loved. When everyone was settled in, happily munching away on the banquet of food that had been assembled, although the plate of Agnes's cheese and chocolate scones was notably untouched, Maggie slipped her arm around Nathan's waist.

"So much has changed so quickly," she said.

"For the better, I hope?" Nathan asked.

Reflecting on the events of the last few weeks, Maggie watched both parts of her family chatting and having fun together. It was everything that had happened since Christmas morning that had really changed her life. Her follow up with Dr Brooks left her grateful that his skill meant he had been able to remove all of her cancer, and hearing that with Nathan at her side, knowing he would be with her no matter what the news was, was a sensation she would never forget. They were going to have to monitor her for a long time to come, but for now, she didn't need any more treatment.

Nathan had received confirmation that the Andersson wanted him, not just for their new hotel as she'd originally thought, but to fit out the penthouses of every single one of their hotels. He was going to be busy for a very long time.

Most importantly, Boxing Day had been spent moving out of the cottage and into the barn. Maggie had booked a moving company to pack all her belongings up and bring them down from London in a couple of months. She was leaving them there for now, in part because a furnished place would make it easier for the estate agents to sell the apartment, but mostly because there was nowhere for her things to go here yet. She and Nathan hoped to get a few more rooms finished before all her stuff turned up.

"Definitely for the better," she said.

"Well, it's not what we imagined; we don't have the helter-skelter, ball pit or princess throne. It's so far from perfect that it's slightly mad," Nathan said, gesturing to the bare stone walls and flooring.

"No, but I couldn't be happier," Maggie said, her heart ready to explode. Standing on tiptoe, she pressed her lips against his. They had taken the long way around, but they were both better for it. This wasn't how they had imagined their future together, but it was everything she wanted.

A NOTE TO THE READER

Dear Reader,

Thank you so much for reading the first Honeyford book. I hope you enjoyed *An Imperfect Christmas*. Whilst each book in the series will be stand alone, there is more to come for the characters of Honeyford. I hope you'll join me as we get to know the wonderful people in this little corner of Somerset better.

Having grown up in such a beautiful part of the country, it was impossible to resist setting the fictional village of Honeyford in Somerset. The fact many of my family still live there simply gives me excellent reasons to visit for further research. I hope you fall in love with the county as much as I did.

I was diagnosed with a rare form of cervical cancer a number of years ago, thankfully, the amazing care from the UK medical services means I am fully recovered. I have always felt a desire to share a little of this experience and feel privileged to be able to do this with you. I fully appreciate that not everyone is as fortunate as I have been in this regard, and my thoughts and wishes are with everyone who is experiencing a tough moment in their journey. I hope that the joy of *An Imperfect Christmas* has provided a little light.

Reviews by readers are incredibly important to authors' success these days, so if you enjoyed the novel and would consider taking the time to leave a review, your efforts would be hugely appreciated. Reviews can be left in many places, but you can access **Amazon** and **Goodreads** here.

I love hearing from readers, and would be delighted if you connected with me through my **Facebook page** via **Twitter** or through my **website**.

Here's to escaping into the pages of more heart-warming lives, and loves, together.

Tanya Jean

www.tanyajeanrussell.com

Sapere Books is an exciting new publisher of brilliant fiction and popular history.

To find out more about our latest releases and our monthly bargain books visit our website:
saperebooks.com

Printed in Poland
by Amazon Fulfillment
Poland Sp. z o.o., Wrocław

65149666R00132